A Shroud for Delilah

A Shroud for
Delilah

ANTHEA FRASER

LUME BOOKS

LUME BOOKS

Published in 2021 by Lume Books
30 Great Guildford Street,
Borough, SE1 0HS

ISBN 978-1-83901-330-0

Typeset using Atomik ePublisher from Easypress Technologies

www.lumebooks.co.uk

CHAPTER 1

When I half-closed my eyes, she looked like Sandra. I'd never noticed it before. They're the same type, of course—selfish, inconsiderate, wanting their own way and not caring who gets hurt. Well, my lady, you won't be hurting anyone else.

God, how her face changed! Polite interest, alarm. Then terror, starting up out of her chair.

And it was so easy! All those nights of sweating and shaking, but when the moment came it meant no more than swatting a fly.

And the look on her face: I keep remembering that…

CHAPTER 2

It was warm in the small room, though the windows were open to the garden. Through them drifted the voices of the children as they played. The scent from the vase of roses was cloyingly sweet, but Madge would be hurt if she pushed it away. Dear Madge, watching her now with the anxious encouragement one reserved for convalescents.

And Kate felt like one: fragile, distanced from reality, like waking from an anaesthetic with the outcome of the operation in doubt.

Madge said quietly, 'What did Michael say, when you told him?'

'He refused to listen. I think it only really sank in this morning.' Memory returned sharply, painfully. Sunlight glinting on the marmalade dish and Michael, in a hurry as usual, frowning up at her.

'Going?' he'd repeated, his tone a mixture of belligerence and disbelief. 'Going where, might I ask?'

Even then, she thought wryly, if he'd stopped to listen, to discuss things calmly, he might have talked her out of it. But he made no attempt to.

'In any case,' he added, with the air of putting an end to her nonsense, 'you can't go anywhere now. Josh starts at St Benedict's next week.'

'Which is where I'm going. To Broadminster, that is. It'll cut out the travelling.'

Michael snorted derisively. 'No doubt you and Madge cooked this up between you. Forgive me if I don't take it seriously.' He glanced at his watch. 'I must be going.'

She had made one last final effort. 'Michael, it's Saturday morning. Surely, in the circumstances, you can spare the time to—'

'News is no respecter of weekends, Kate. You knew that when you married me. It's too late to complain now.'

'Yes,' she agreed flatly. 'It's too late.'

He darted a quick look at her and pushed back his chair. 'I can't stop now. We'll talk about it this evening.'

'But I shan't—' she began, and broke off as Josh wandered into the room. Michael ruffled his hair on the way out and a moment later the front door closed behind him.

Madge watched the emotions cross her friend's face. Had she done right, helping Kate find work and accommodation here? Paul didn't think so. 'Keep out of it,' he'd advised. 'Left to themselves they'll sort something out.' But she couldn't refuse Kate's plea for help. They'd been friends since their first day at school, and in today's vulnerability Madge saw the bewildered child of twenty-five years ago.

She couldn't imagine why Kate had left Michael. He was abrasive, clever, and intolerant, but Kate adored him. And despite their many shared secrets, there'd been no hint of marital trouble, a loyalty Madge understood.

'We'd no idea there was anything wrong,' she said.

Kate's eyes flickered as she came back to the present. 'I hoped it would blow over, but it didn't. It's not a sudden decision, Madge. Things have been getting worse for months. Then the usual kind person told me he'd been seen with a girl. I didn't believe it at first, but people started making veiled comments so I tackled him about it. He flew off the handle and accused me of listening to gossip, but when I persisted he said the girl was a colleague on the paper, and did I grudge him a little relaxation? He seemed to forget he used to relax at home.' She was silent, staring down at her clasped hands. 'The crunch came when Josh and I bumped into them.'

'Oh, Kate!'

'Josh was taking part in a sponsored swim. He wanted us to go and support him, but Michael said he was too tied up with this murder story.'

'And wasn't he?'

'I doubt if there were any corpses in the Red Lion, which is where he'd apparently spent the evening. We were just passing when they came out with their arms round each other.'

She stood up and walked to the window, staring out at the long, narrow garden and the children playing in it. Josh and Tim were up the apple tree, Donna dancing impatiently beneath. The scene had a golden, timeless quality about it, suffused with the late-summer sunshine of remembered childhood, and fleetingly it could have been herself and her two cousins playing there. Kate shook her head to clear it.

'Which,' she said without turning, 'was when I phoned you, and, as always, you came to the rescue.'

'It was a piece of luck hearing the same day that Molly was leaving Pennyfarthings.'

'Did she live in the flat too?'

'No, she was local. Wangling the flat took a bit more doing. They use it as a showroom and for entertaining, but when I explained the position, Mr .Bailey agreed. What did you think of him, by the way?'

Kate turned from the window, and to Madge's relief her smile was less strained. 'Quite the ladies' man, isn't he?'

'Given the chance, but his wings have been clipped. Molly said his girlfriend's moved in with him.' Madge looked up at the clock. 'I'll put the kettle on; Paul should be back any minute.'

The local paper lay on the table and Kate picked it up, automatically assessing the layout. The front page was devoted to the murder which had made national headlines.

'Stalemate on "Delilah,"' she read. 'There have been no new developments in the case of divorcée Linda Meadowes, found stabbed at her Shillingham home two weeks ago. In his column this week Michael Romilly, an acquaintance of the dead woman, considers the implications of her murder.'

Madge came back as Kate dropped the paper onto the table. 'I hadn't realized Michael knew the woman.'

'Only casually, but that's why he's following it up himself.'

'What was she like?'

'A bit flighty. She and two men were had up recently for causing a disturbance, and neither was the man she was living with.'

'Delilah indeed! Still, she didn't deserve to die.'

The sound of the front door reached them, and Paul came into the room. Tall, thin, and bespectacled, there was an air of dependability about him which today struck Kate more forcibly than ever. He gave her a quick hug and patted her shoulder.

'Good to see you, Kate, though I'm sorry about the circumstances. Where's my godson?'

'Up the apple tree, when last seen.'

Paul felt for his pipe, not looking at her. 'How's all this affecting him?'

'Not at all, so far. I explained it was easier to live here once he starts at St Benedict's, but that Michael couldn't because of his job.'

'And he accepted it?'

'Yes. We don't see much of Michael anyway.'

It had been Paul, a master at the school, who suggested they send Josh to St Benedict's. Traditionally it supplied choristers for the Minster and Josh's clear, sweet treble had helped to secure him a place.

'I'll call the children in for tea,' Madge said.

Josh, taking his place at the kitchen table, was flushed and bright-eyed from play, giving no hint of dismay at his uprooting. But this house was his second home, and its familiarity soothed Kate too on this day of displacement—the clock ticking on the wall, the row of wilting plants Madge always forgot to water. They had had tea here so often that it was hard to accept that this occasion was any different from the others. She felt a burst of gratitude for them all, looking affectionately round the table at Paul, and young Tim with the brace on his teeth, and Donna, small and ponytailed, intent on her tea. And especially at Madge. During their schooldays, she had reminded Kate of a small brown bird, and she'd hardly changed. Her hair was still smooth and glossy, her eyes bright, and the soft roundness of contented motherhood merely intensified the impression. Kate wondered what she'd have done without them.

After the meal, Paul suggested they walk back to the flat with her. 'There's no parking in Monks' Walk so you'd better leave the car here till you find out where you can garage it.'

Monks' Walk was the historic heart of Broadminster. Basically it formed a crescent curving round three sides of the Minster and its wide expanse of Green. Coming from the Netherbys' house, they joined it two thirds of the way along. To their right, the eastern section swept round towards St Benedict's and Broad Street, one of the busier thoroughfares of the town, while on their left, its ancient houses a hotchpotch of differing styles, lay the centre block where Kate would be living. Though the majority of the buildings were three-storeyed, they presented anything but a uniform skyline, being a wide variety of shapes and heights. At ground level, most of them housed boutiques, art galleries, and coffeehouses. And facing them across the Green, the majestic lines of Broad Minster soared to the sky.

'Don't expect a lie-in on Sundays!' Paul warned with a grin. 'Once the bells start, there's no point in staying in bed.'

'Here we are.' Kate stopped at a glass-paned door immediately next to the antique shop. 'As you see, we have our private entrance.'

The linoleumed passageway smelt of polish. There was a door in the right-hand wall and another, glass-paned, at the far end, giving access to a courtyard behind the premises. Just short of it, a flight of stairs led upwards.

'What's behind here?' Madge asked, tapping the interior door as she passed.

'The office at the back of the shop. It'll save me getting wet when it rains.'

They followed her up the stairs and looked about them. A fair-sized living room took up most of the floor space but at the back of the room a counter separated it from the kitchen area. Mullioned windows at the front looked directly out to the Minster. The room was plainly but attractively decorated, a perfect foil for the large watercolours hanging on the walls and the handsome chairs and tables with which it was furnished.

'It'll be like living in a museum,' Madge said a little doubtfully.

'Some of the delicate things have been put away, but Josh is very careful. I don't think he'll damage anything.'

'It's the more modern trappings that interest him,' Paul commented as Josh and the other children, having switched on the television, flopped to the floor in front of it.

'At least you have modern plumbing.' Madge had turned her attention to the kitchen. 'You never know, with these old buildings. Oh, and look, Kate, at the lovely little courtyard down here.'

She was peering out of the window, and Kate and Paul joined her. The walled yard below was imaginatively adorned with tubs of ornamental trees and shrubs. In one corner a couple of iron tables were piled on each other against the wall and a garden umbrella drooped over them.

'Would you like to see upstairs?'

Paul and Madge followed Kate up the second flight of stairs, where three doors opened off a tiny landing. The main bedroom ran along the front of the building. A second, much smaller, was next to it, and the bathroom at the stair head.

'Small but adequate,' Kate said brightly, feeling like an estate agent.

'Does Michael know where you are?' Paul asked.

She coloured. 'That we're in Broadminster, that's all. He didn't show any interest, but if he wants us, no doubt he'll contact you.'

'You're quite sure about this, Kate? Taking the flat makes it seem rather permanent.' He glanced accusingly at his wife.

'We have to live somewhere,' Kate said defiantly, 'whether for three weeks or three months. I had to get away, Paul,' she added in a low voice. 'Madge will explain.'

'As long as you know what you're doing. But if you'd like me to ring Michael and ask him to come and fetch you, I'd be only too happy.'

Kate shook her head and started back down the stairs. Madge gave her husband a warning look and followed her. 'How about coming to lunch tomorrow?' she suggested as they reached the living area.

'Bless you, but no. I want to get everything straight before starting work on Monday.'

'Josh had better spend his time with us till school starts. You won't want him under your feet, and Tim'll be glad of his company.'

Shortly afterwards the Netherbys left. Kate and Josh stood at the window till the bend of the crescent hid them from view and she turned away, suddenly overwhelmed by what she had done. Would Michael have arrived home yet, and be surprised to find her gone?

As though catching the echo of her thoughts, Josh broke into them. 'Will Daddy be coming tomorrow?'

Kate switched on a smile she hoped he was too young to analyse. 'I shouldn't think so, as soon as this. He's very busy at the moment.'

He accepted her answer without comment, extracting a toy car from his pocket and starting to run it along the windowsill.

'Don't scratch the paint,' she said mechanically. She looked with love at the toffee-coloured hair and large candid eyes, obscurely grateful that he resembled neither Michael nor herself, though his quick frown as the toy fell to the floor was undeniably his father's.

'Come along, then,' she said briskly, 'you can help me unpack.'

Two hours later the flat was tidy and Josh asleep in his little room. Kate made herself some coffee and walked with it to the window. For some minutes she stood staring across at the Minster until a movement in the street below distracted her. Tilting her head, she could make out two figures straining together in the shadows and she moved back in case they should see her. 'Don't cry, young lovers, whoever you are; don't cry because I'm alone.'

She turned away and switched on the television, but her mind refused to register it. Now she and Josh had gone, there'd be nothing to keep Michael from his girl. Jealousy twisted her stomach as his image blazed across her mind—lean face, impatient mouth, alert dark eyes. Though she accepted that enjoyment of each other's bodies no longer outweighed the mental hurt, she knew that should Michael walk into the room, she'd go to him. Knew it, and despised herself.

Wearily, drained by the pressures of the day, she went upstairs. The narrow room was stuffy, the day's sunshine stored beneath its sloping ceiling. Kate pushed up the sash window. From this height the Minster was still visible against its background of trees, but the parapet which edged the building shut off everything below. An ivory tower, she thought.

She had made up the bed earlier with linen from the spare room in Shillingham, and the bedspread looked oddly familiar in its alien setting. The floorboards were polished and a sheepskin rug lay beside the bed. Adequate, as she'd assured Madge and Paul.

She crossed to the dressing table and, leaning forward, studied her reflection. Her short dark hair fell as usual in soft curls over her forehead, and the large eyes Michael had laughingly described as navy-blue stared solemnly back at her. The traumatic day had left surprisingly little mark.

With a sigh she straightened and started to undress.

CHAPTER 3

Detective Chief Inspector Webb switched on the ignition and the car moved slowly forward. It was a hell of a way to start a week. In the last twenty-four hours he had attained his forty-sixth birthday, upset Hannah, and received news of another murder. And, for good measure, it was pouring with rain.

Another murder, for God's sake. Down in Broadminster this time, but the M.O. tied in with the Meadowes case, which landed it neatly in his lap. And they hadn't got anywhere with the first one yet. Nearly two weeks of searching, interviewing, house-to-house inquiries, and they were no nearer murderer or motive than when they'd started.

The traffic lights at the foot of the hill turned red as he approached and he swore briefly, reaching up to adjust the rear-view mirror. Starkly the glass gave back his reflection: plentiful brown hair, hard mouth, bleak grey eyes.

So what had they got so far? Not a lot, he thought with grim humour, and what they had was mostly negative. No break-in, no robbery, no murder weapon. The victim had been in her own armchair, stabbed once through the heart. Nothing out of place—except for the scrawled word 'Delilah' in lipstick on the mirror. A bizarre touch, that, almost as shocking in the neat little room as the corpse herself, seated comfortably in her chair.

Webb frowned and, as the lights changed, inched the car forward. No clue there, either. The tube of lipstick, discarded on the hearthrug, had proved to be the dead woman's, and hers were the only prints on it.

Weaving his way in and out of the early traffic, he mentally reviewed the suspects. First the cohabitant Robert Preston, who had a cast-iron alibi in the shape of a factory full of workmates. No way he could have slipped out to stab his lady-friend, even if he'd wanted to. Then the two she'd been in court with the week before her death. Nix again. Blake was a commercial traveller, in Cardiff at the crucial time. And Kittle, a bus driver, had been on duty. The ex-husband Don Meadowes, while there were certain ambiguities in his statement, had no motive that Webb could see. He seemed glad to be rid of Linda and planning to make an honest woman of the girl he was now shacked up with.

The Chief Inspector sighed and turned into the broad, rain-washed thoroughfare of Carrington Street. Halfway along it, set back from the road, was Shillingham Police Station, a modern building fronted by a circle of lawn in the centre of which was a large pond. On less fraught occasions, Webb sometimes paused by it on his way to lunch, the artist in him marvelling at the waxy perfection of the lilies that floated there, rose-pink and golden and white, among the shiny green mat of their leaves. But this morning he had no time for floral appreciation. As he circled the grass he was watching out for Jackson, who came hurrying down the steps as he drew up, shoulders hunched against the rain.

'Morning, Governor. You want to drive?'

'Yes, I'll carry on.'

Jackson settled himself in the passenger seat, smoothing his hands over his thinning sandy hair to remove the rain. Under their jutting brows his china-blue eyes were alive with anticipation.

'Looks like we're off again.'

'Seems so. You've got the directions?'

'Yes, the report was waiting.'

'Let's have it, then.' Webb glanced over his shoulder, edged out again into the mainstream of traffic.

'Firstly, Stonebridge want you to report in once you've sized everything up.'

Webb grunted. He'd guessed Headquarters would come in on this. 'What's the form?'

The Sergeant fumbled inside his raincoat and extracted a sheet of paper. 'Court Lane phoned through at o-eight-o-five. Body of a woman aged about forty discovered by her sister just after seven-thirty.'

'Was the sister living with her?'

'No, they were due to go on holiday today. She arrived as arranged and found the door on the latch. Thought her sister'd left it ready for her and went in all unsuspecting.'

'And they think our chap's responsible?'

'It's the writing on the mirror. "Delilah," same as last time.'

'Bloody hell.'

They said little more during the drive, each busy with his own thoughts. The countryside was obscured by a haze of drizzle, misty in the distance, opaque and glistening nearer at hand. Cows stood dejectedly in the fields and cyclists battled along with heads down, their yellow capes billowing out behind them.

Only as they approached the outskirts of Broadminster and the first set of traffic lights halted their progress did Webb rouse himself. 'Where are we heading?'

'Larchwood Lane. We'll have to go through the town; it's off Lower Broad Street,' Fenton said. 'I've brought the street map.' He unfolded it, tracing the route. 'Yes, here we are. Down past the hospital, first exit at the roundabout, and it's the second turning on the right.'

Larchwood Lane was a fairly recent development of some two dozen houses built to a chalet design. Already the wooden boardings were beginning to fade but the deep eaves and white paintwork still looked attractive. As implied, the *cul-de-sac* ended in a small wood.

This Monday morning, the quiet backwater was a hive of excitement. An ambulance was parked at the gate of No. 15 awaiting clearance to remove the body. In front and behind it, a motley collection of cars and vans had drawn up, and the uniformed constable on guard at the gate was surrounded by a group of journalists and photographers.

Webb drew in behind the end car and got out. The rain had stopped and there was a pungent smell of wet leaves. On the opposite pavement a small crowd had gathered, women with shopping baskets, young mothers with prams, a couple of men self-consciously on the fringe, hands in pockets. Embarrassed, somehow ashamed of their curiosity, they looked away as he glanced in their direction.

The waiting newsmen had no such inhibitions. '*Broadshire News*, sir. Can you give us any details?'

With the ease born of long practice, Webb shouldered his way past. 'I haven't any myself yet, gentlemen. You'll have a statement in due course.'

'But can you confirm that this murder is linked with—?'

Nodding to the constable on the gate, Webb strode up the path, Jackson at his heels. They made an odd pair, the Chief Inspector tall and lanky, the Sergeant by contrast short and slight. Some wit at Headquarters had dubbed them Dignity and Impudence, but the sobriquets did not concern them. They respected each other, knew the workings of each other's mind, and together presented a formidable combination, as many a villain had found to his cost.

'Morning, Dave. Nice little present we've got for you.'

The man who came to meet them was tall and broad-shouldered, with a hooked nose and shaggy dark hair. Not for the first time, Jackson reflected that Chief D.I. Horn looked more like a con man than a detective.

'Hello, Foggy. What's the score?'

'Not much to go on so far. I was first on the scene—live just round the corner. Had a quick look to confirm death, otherwise no one's been in except Doc Roscoe and the scenes-of-crime boys. They've moved out to let the pathologist do his stuff—he's in there now. It's Stapleton, from Broadshire General. He's got a string of PMs lined up for this morning and wasn't prepared to hang around. Time of death provisionally estimated as yesterday afternoon, and the M.O. seems the same as your Shillingham bloke. Think he's spreading his wings?'

'Sounds like it, unless we're in for a spate of copycat crimes. I'll have a quick look myself before the boys move back.'

He ducked his head as he went through the low doorway.

A square hall lay ahead, with an open kitchen door at the end. Already there was a faintly unpleasant smell in the house. It had been a warm night. The door on the left was ajar and Webb eased it open with his foot, surveying the scene inside. A stone fireplace took up most of one wall, the empty grate screened with leaves and grasses. On a low table lay some knitting and one of the popular Sunday papers, open at the television programmes. Dr Stapleton was standing in the middle of the room thoughtfully studying the limp body in an easy chair. Briefly Webb's eyes went beyond him to the red letters scrawled across the mirror. They looked depressingly familiar.

He introduced himself and the pathologist nodded. He was a small man with a dried-out air about him. His hands and feet were small and neat as a woman's and he wore rimless spectacles.

'From a purely visual examination, Chief Inspector, death appears to have been caused by circulatory shock due to a stab wound. What interests me is the cadaveric spasm.' He nodded towards the hands, convulsively gripping the arms of the chair. 'No attempt at self-defence, it seems. She must have died extremely quickly.'

Webb stood looking down at the dead woman. She was fair-haired, might even have been pretty, but a latent insipidity had been cruelly emphasized by the vacuity of death. Through her open sandals he could see that the toenails were painted bright pink—ready, no doubt, for the beaches of Benidorm or wherever. Webb sighed. That small vanity made the woman suddenly more real, the fact of her death more depressing. A tube of lipstick lay at her feet, presumably removed after death from the open handbag. If it followed the Meadowes case, there'd be no prints on it but the dead woman's.

17

Dr Stapleton cleared his throat. 'Well, I've finished here, Chief Inspector. Can't say any more till I get her on the slab. I'll let you have a report as soon as I can.'

While Webb was inspecting the scene, Jackson waited outside the front door. Over by the hedge, a couple of men were methodically pulling aside the heavy bushes in their search for the murder weapon, swearing as the tangled branches drenched their sleeves. Across the road he could see a detective talking to a woman at her door. A thrush was chirruping on the low eave above his head. Little did it know there would be no more bacon rinds from this address.

The constable at the gate turned and, seeing Jackson standing there, ambled up the path. He jerked his head towards the house. 'That the one they call "Spiderman"?'

Jackson grinned. 'That's him.'

'Why's that, then?'

'His name, I suppose. Webb, Spider. One of the old lags started it and it spread. "Will you come into my parlour," and all that.'

'Going to take over, is he? From Chief D.I. Horn?'

Jackson shrugged. 'If you ask me, Stonebridge will come in now. They're waiting for the Governor to report back.'

The sound of approaching voices sent the constable quickly back to his post. He'd just reached it when the pathologist appeared, followed by Webb. Stapleton nodded to Horn, who was chatting to the scenes-of-crime officers, walked briskly down the path and got into his car.

Horn joined Webb at the front door. 'OK if the boys carry on?'

'Yes, of course.' Webb stood to one side while the two men moved back inside. 'What's her name, by the way?'

'Patricia Burke. Mrs.'

'Husband in evidence?'

'No, her divorce was finalized last week. That's why she and her sister were going away, to give her a break.'

'You saw the sister, didn't you. How did she seem?'

'Incoherent. All I could get out of her was that she had two tickets for the ferry. Kept asking how she could cancel them. Odd, the things the mind fastens on in times of shock.'

'She's at Court Lane?'

'Yes, a WDC collected her. The doctor will have seen her by now, but I doubt if she's fit to be interviewed.'

'Wonder how close they were, whether she knew her sister's friends, and so on. If we could establish a connection between this woman and Linda Meadowes, we could be onto something. Even though they lived twenty miles apart, they seem to have had at least one friend in common—if you could call him that.'

'We might learn something from the neighbours. The support group are doing a house-to-house now and as you can see we've started searching the grounds. No point getting the dogs in, though. The scent'll be cold by now and the rain won't have helped either. Likewise, roadblocks are a waste of time. Our man could be halfway round the world by now. Think how many flights have left Heathrow in the last eighteen hours.'

'All the same, Foggy, it's my bet he's sitting pretty not too far away, watching with interest to see what we'll do.'

One of the support group turned in at the gate and Horn went down to talk to him. The garden was bright with the recent rain, the soil rich and dark, the grass silver-bladed as a watery sun struggled from behind the clouds. Webb looked round for Jackson. He was standing at the front window, watching the

19

men at work inside. Webb joined him. The pleasant room, with a television in the corner and the knitting on the table, was an unlikely setting for murder, an uncannily accurate repeat of the Meadowes case. Perhaps because of his jaundiced mood today, the whole affair disturbed him. He had the feeling they were in for trouble with Mr Delilah.

'I don't like it, Ken,' he commented. 'All right, so we can accept that a man can be let down so badly that he wants to kill—*does* kill, in fact, and labels the woman "Delilah" to make his point. Fair enough. But *another* woman? The same man? It makes nonsense of the motives—dilutes the whole thing. He couldn't have been involved enough with two women at the same time, both of whom let him down badly enough to get themselves killed.'

'Unless he's a modern Bluebeard suffering the effects of Women's Lib!' Jackson grinned. 'In which case,' he added, 'we could be in for a whole string of them!'

Which was altogether too close to the way Webb's own mind had been running. 'A regular ray of sunshine you are!' he said bitterly, and went in search of Horn.

CHAPTER 4

When Kate and Josh came downstairs that Monday morning, the door leading to the office stood open and through it they could see Bailey studying a catalogue. He looked up with a smile.

'Come in, Mrs Romilly. Settling in all right? Hello, young fellow! I didn't realize we had two new assistants!'

'I hope you don't mind,' Kate apologized. 'He doesn't start school till Thursday and I didn't like to leave him alone. Madge Netherby's collecting him at ten, and he's promised to sit quietly till then. This is Mr Bailey, Josh.'

'No problem at all, and welcome to Pennyfarthings. It's a blessing you could step in like this. Molly's husband was offered a post in the States and they flew out almost at once.'

'It was lucky for me, too.'

Out in the shop the doorbell chimed and a woman came hurrying through to the office drawing off her gloves.

'I'm so sorry, Mr Bailey. The bus was late again.'

He waved aside her apologies. 'Lana, this is Mrs Romilly, who's come to work with us. Miss Truscott, our secretary, book-keeper, and general factotum.'

The woman smiled shyly at Kate, murmured a response to her greeting, and, drawing the cover off her typewriter, sat down and began to open the mail. Kate saw she was younger than her first impression indicated—mid thirties, probably, though her severe hairstyle and the fine skin drawn tautly over her face made her seem older. She looked up to meet Josh's unblinking gaze, and her expression softened.

'Good morning. And what's your name?'

'Josh Romilly. I'm going to St Benedict's on Thursday.'

'Are you, indeed? Does that mean you can sing?'

'Oh yes. I was the solo at the end of term concert. At Highfield, that was.' He moved towards her, fingering the flex of the type-writer. 'How does that work?'

'Josh, you promised—'

'He doesn't worry me,' Lana Truscott put in quickly.

'In that case,' Bailey said, rising to his feet, 'I'll show Mrs Romilly round while you two get to know each other.'

Kate had only a confused memory of the shop from her interview the previous week. Now she was glad to walk slowly round, inspecting with interest the ornate vases and delicately carved chairs which stood in seeming harmony with more modern pieces.

'As you see, we're not strictly an antique shop,' her employer was saying. 'We do have some valuable things—signed prints, *objets d'art* and so on, but we also stock good modern stuff, to lure the discerning tourist.' He paused, indicating an alcove stacked with shelves and fronted by tables bearing an assortment of coins, small pieces of silver, and porcelain.

'We call this Collector's Corner. All these will appreciate in value. My partner spends most of his time scouring the country for suitable stock. That dagger, for instance.' He pointed to a long, slim weapon made entirely of steel, the hilt covered with ornate gold damascening. 'Comes from India, mid-nineteenth-century, and there's a smaller dagger concealed in the hilt. Clever, isn't it? Richard's really into swords and such. He has quite a collection at home. Personally, these snuffboxes are more my line of country. Aren't they exquisite? But of course—I was forgetting!' He flashed her an easy smile. 'You probably know as much as I do. You've a History of Art degree, haven't you?'

'I've not done much with it, I'm afraid. I married straight from university and Josh was born a year later. It's only since he started school that I've taken it up again.'

The doorbell sounded and the first customer of the day stepped hesitantly inside. Beaming reassurance, Bailey went to greet him, and Kate, feeling *de trop*, retreated to the office to see what Josh was doing. She needn't have worried; he'd drawn a chair up to the desk and was contentedly scribbling on a piece of paper. In the courtyard outside a crowd of sparrows fluttered and squawked over a freshly filled bird tray.

'One of my first jobs each morning!' Miss Truscott said, following Kate's gaze. 'Josh helped me today. I hope you haven't a cat, Mrs Romilly.'

'Somebody wanting prints of old cars,' Bailey said as he came back. 'Which reminds me, where did you leave your car?'

'At the Netherbys' for the moment. I didn't know what to do with it.'

'I should have explained—there's a residents' car park in Lady Ann Square. You'll need a permit but that shouldn't be a problem. Do you know Broadminster?'

'Only from visits to Madge.'

'You'll soon find your way around.'

As promised, Madge collected Josh at ten o'clock. Lana Truscott seemed sorry to see him go. 'He's an intelligent little boy, isn't he?' she commented. 'You must be very proud of him.'

The morning passed slowly. Kate started to unpack some ornaments in the stockroom at the back of the shop. There weren't many customers. Monday morning did not seem a propitious time to buy antiques.

'There aren't enough of us to stagger lunch hours,' Bailey told her at twelve-thirty. 'Lana only works mornings and I'm not always here, so it's easier to close. As it's your first day I'll treat you to a pub lunch.'

Kate was taken aback. 'It's kind of you, but I was going to do some shopping. There are several things—'

'Plenty of time, we're closed till two.'

'Then thank you. I hadn't realized Miss Truscott only works part time,' she added as Bailey locked up behind them.

'She lives with her invalid father and he needs a lot of attention.'

The Green was dotted with groups of office workers eating their lunch, while behind them the ancient Minster dried itself in the sun. Farther along Monks' Walk a bow-fronted shop was doing a brisk trade in takeaway snacks.

'*Plus ça change,*' Bailey said with a smile. 'It was a coffee-house two hundred years ago and still is, though it's moved with the times. Pizzas rather than seed cakes these days.'

They turned down a cobbled lane leading to the High Street. 'We'll go to the Coach and Horses. It's near the market and you can do your shopping after we've eaten.'

As he lounged at the counter awaiting their order, Kate studied her employer critically. His thick, curly hair, prematurely grey, had the paradoxical effect of making his face boyish. He smiled frequently, showing even white teeth in a tanned face, and she suspected uncharitably that he'd been told he was charming and couldn't forget it. Of average height, his figure already showed the first signs of too many pub lunches. Wryly, she wondered what opinion he had formed of her.

'Here we are, then. I'm quite hungry—we slept in this morning and hadn't time for breakfast.'

Kate wondered if she was supposed to know his domestic arrangements but he solved the problem for her.

'My girlfriend's a model and lives largely on air, so she had no sympathy. Said it would do me good to skip a few meals!' He patted his thickening waist ruefully and Kate found herself warming to him.

'What does she model?'

'Nella? Herself, mostly. That is, not specifically clothes, though she does on occasion. You've probably seen her in the glossies - in the latest car, the most modern kitchen, the nattiest cruiser.'

'Doesn't it give her expensive tastes?'

'Yes, but also the means to indulge them.'

He glanced across at her. 'I'm sorry about your marriage.'

'Thank you.'

'Mrs Netherby wasn't specific. Is it a temporary separation?'

'I rather doubt it.'

'Well, there's a lot of it about. Divorce, I mean. One reason why I'm not anxious to take the plunge. I saw what it did to Richard.'

'Your partner?'

He nodded. 'He and his wife split up a couple of years ago. She resented his being away so much, there were no children to complicate things, so she upped and left. It knocked him sideways for a while.'

Kate said drily, 'Yes, children do complicate things.'

'I was impressed by your son. Bright kid, I should say.'

'Bright enough.' She pushed her plate away. 'Thank you, Mr Bailey. I enjoyed that.'

'I think we might stretch to first names, don't you? It makes it easier working together. I answer to Martin.'

'Kate.'

'It suits you. Lana, of course, persists in calling me "Mr Bailey," so I've given up on that. She's old-fashioned in a lot of ways. Unmarried, of course.'

'Like you!' Kate said wickedly, and he gave a shout of laughter.

'*Touché*! A chauvinistic remark, if I ever heard one! Like Nella too, come to that, but there the resemblance ends. Still, Lana's worth her weight in gold. She has a way with children, too. Yours took to her, didn't he? Classic case of a mother *manqué*.' He consulted his watch. 'Well, if you want to buy some groceries we'd better make a move. I'm expecting a long-distance call at two.'

There were still a large number of tourists in Broadminster, and American voices echoed through the narrow streets. The indoor market was very rewarding. Kate filled her basket with cheeses and herbs, freshly baked bread and glowing fruit while Martin moved round inspecting the second-hand bookstall and chatting with the stall-holders. He seemed to know them all.

During the course of the afternoon Kate made her first sale, a seventeenth-century map of Broadshire.

'Your customer was so excited, he forgot his paper,' Martin said, picking it up from the counter. 'The evening one, too— he must only just have bought it.' His voice changed as he unfolded it. 'My God, another murder! Did you bring your Shillingham killer with you?'

He spread the paper on the counter and Kate leaned over his shoulder. 'Delilah killer in Broadminster?' she read, and her eyes raced down the columns. 'Granted a divorce only last week— killed yesterday afternoon—lipstick writing on the mirror.'

'How horrible,' she said softly.

'A bit close to home, certainly.'

'Michael had met the other woman.'

'Michael?'

'My husband.'

Martin turned to look at her. 'Michael—Romilly? Michael Romilly's your husband? Of course—it never struck me. I always read his articles—first-class stuff. Quite brilliant.'

Oh, he's brilliant, Kate agreed silently. And cynical, and sarcastic, and impatient of other people's opinions, which didn't make him easy to live with. Nonetheless, she was missing the stimulus of his conversation, his lightning assessment of political figures, his thumbnail sketches which brought a scene or person instantly to life. Whatever else life had been with Michael, it was never dull.

'You say he knew the first victim?'

'Not well, but he'd met her once or twice. In pubs, I think.'

'I wonder if there's any connection between her and this latest one. Sunday afternoon. It sounds so peaceful, doesn't it, especially in your own home. You're relaxing with the papers after lunch, there's a knock at the door and—*finito*. Curtains.'

Kate shivered. 'You wouldn't think she'd let anyone in, with the papers full of the other case.'

Where was she, when that poor woman was killed? She and Josh had gone for a walk—they might even have passed the murderer! The idea was absurd, impossible. Yet not impossible. She realized suddenly that the murder would have brought Michael to Broadminster. Had he been round to Madge's and found Josh?

'Five o'clock.' Martin's voice broke into her thoughts. 'Lock up, will you, Kate? And here's the passage door key, you might as well take charge of it. If your doorbell rings, for God's sake don't answer it!' He was only half-joking, and Kate's mouth was dry.

When he'd gone, she went out to the courtyard to check that the gate was locked. There was no key, but it was secured with bolts top and bottom. She looked up at the wall. No one could climb that, and since the house was attached to its neighbours, only the front was unprotected.

With an effort she pulled herself together. People were murdered all the time, unfortunately, and she hadn't been neurotic about it before. But nor had she been alone before, or had a link, however tenuous, with one of the victims.

Pushing such thoughts from her mind, she went to Mead Way to collect Josh. Madge opened the door.

'Have you seen the evening paper?'

Kate nodded. 'Was Michael here?'

'No, I was half-expecting him, but he never appeared.'

'And he hasn't phoned?'

'Not a peep.'

Kate should have felt relieved, but perversely she didn't. Wasn't he anxious about her, alone in the town where a woman had been murdered? Or had he completely washed his hands of her?

'The children are watching telly. Have you time for a cup of tea?'

'I'd love one.'

The familiar kitchen again, with the Monday pile of ironing and a smell of stew coming from the oven.

'Where's Paul?'

'He had a staff meeting this afternoon. Tying up loose ends before term starts on Thursday.'

Lucky Madge, to be expecting her husband home and the prospect of a safe, normal evening ahead. A shared meal, desultory conversation, bed. And if she woke in the night dreaming of murder, she could nestle against Paul and go back to sleep.

As I could with Michael, Kate reminded herself. If she was beginning to think that way after two days, there was nothing to stop her crawling back—if he'd have her.

She could even keep the job: drive down with Josh every morning, work at Penny-farthings, and take him back in the evening. 'Kate?'

'Sorry, I was miles away.'

'I was asking how work went?'

'Oh, I actually made a sale. One of those lovely, yellowing old maps. I'd have liked it myself.'

'That's a good start.' Madge poured the tea from the comfortable brown pot. Safe—normal—comfortable. Why were these the adjectives that kept occurring to her? Kate wondered impatiently.

'Josh can come tomorrow too, if it helps.'

Kate roused herself. 'Wouldn't he be a nuisance?'

'Of course not. Tim's delighted to have him so near, and I've had the least interrupted day I can remember.'

'Then bless you. Miss Truscott was very kind, but her patience might wear thin after a whole day of him. We can reciprocate at the weekend.'

Madge looked at her quickly. 'Won't Michael be down?'

'Perhaps. If he's not too busy.' She was ashamed of the bitterness in her voice.

'We'll see how it goes,' Madge said placatingly.

Accordingly, Josh was collected again the next morning, and soon after, Martin left to keep an appointment. The steady typing from the office advised against interruption, so Kate took a duster and busied herself with some cleaning.

The sound of the door brought her round some shelves face to face with an unusual customer. The girl who had entered would have made an impact anywhere; in the rarefied atmosphere of Pennyfarthings, the effect was startling. Her hair was gold and her eyes deep violet, lustrously, and probably falsely, lashed. She wore parrot-green cords, high-heeled gold sandals, and a turquoise blouse of pure silk with the sleeves carelessly rolled up. An assortment of gold chains hung round her neck, her wrists, and both ankles.

Kate said tentatively, 'Good morning. Can I help you?'

'You're Kate,' the girl stated. 'I'm Nella Cavendish.'

'Ah—yes, of course.' Martin's girlfriend. She took the hand thrust towards her and met the assessing violet eyes, adding awkwardly, 'How do you do?'

'Martin told me he'd taken you to lunch, so I thought I'd better come and inspect you.'

'Do I pass muster?'

To her surprise, Nella took the question seriously. 'I think he fancies you. Should I feel threatened?'

Kate stared at her. 'I'm—not sure what you mean.'

'Well, you've left your husband, haven't you, and Martin seems interested. I wondered if you'd any designs on him.'

Kate drew in her breath. 'You don't mince words, do you?'

'I like to clear the air.'

'Apparently. Well, you can rest assured. I've no plans to get my hooks into Martin.'

'You see, there's nothing I could do about it, if he wanted to be hooked. That's the trouble with this no-strings arrangement. You're never quite sure how permanent you are.'

Kate, who hadn't realized the word permanent could be qualified, felt a stirring of pity. For all her brazenness and her dramatic appearance, there was something insecure about Nella. She wondered if the girl really loved Martin, would have welcomed a more conventional setup. But as though answering her thought, Nella added carelessly, 'Of course, it works both ways. He's not too happy when I spend the weekend with a crowd of randy photographers, but there's nothing he can do, either.' She gave a laugh. 'At least we never take each other for granted.'

There was a pause. 'Would you like some coffee?' Kate inquired.

'Not if I have to face the old bat. She thinks I'm a bad lot. Not Martin, of course. Men can do as they like in her eyes. She doesn't seem to realize they need girls to do it with! Still, I approve of her. I wish all Martin's acquaintances looked like Miss Truscott!'

'I'm sure you needn't worry,' Kate reassured her. 'He seems very proud of you.'

The lovely face brightened. 'Does he? Good. Sorry to grill you like this, but it's better to know from the beginning where you stand. You must come round for supper one evening.'

'A lettuce leaf?' queried Kate, and Nella laughed.

'Don't worry, I'm a good cook when I bother, even if of the "dash of that and handful of this" variety. I have flair.'

'I can believe it.'

'I mustn't take up any more of your time. I've a booking at eleven, anyway. Glad to have met you, Kate.' And she swung round and left as suddenly as she'd appeared.

Thoughtfully Kate went into the office. 'Shall I make some coffee?'

Lana looked up. 'I'm sorry, I hadn't realized it was so late. I'll get it now.'

Ignoring her offer, Kate filled the kettle and plugged it in. 'I've just met Miss Nella Cavendish.'

'Oh yes?' A flush spread over her pale skin. 'She's very colourful, isn't she?'

'Flamboyant would be a better word. Still, it's not my place to criticize.' She sounded like a Victorian housekeeper, born, perhaps, a century too late. Waiting for the kettle, Kate studied the scraped-back hair and unadorned face. If she'd only take an interest in herself, Miss Truscott might well surprise people. Her bone structure was delicate, her skin flawless, and her eyes, when they could be tricked into meeting yours, were hauntingly beautiful.

The kettle whistled shrilly and she poured the water into the mugs. As she set Lana's down by the typewriter, the woman said, 'I was telling my father about your little boy. He'd so like to meet him. Do you think—I mean, would you mind if I took him home one afternoon, for tea? I'd bring him back well before bedtime.'

'That's kind of you,' Kate said slowly, and Lana, misinterpreting her hesitation, added quickly, 'There's nothing unpleasant in Father's appearance. Nothing that could frighten Josh. And the little boy next door has rabbits—I'm sure he'd enjoy playing

with them. I could bake a cake and make some sandwiches—'
She looked up, eyes pleading now. Her breath smelt, disconcertingly, of bread and butter—or perhaps it was association of ideas.

'I'm sure he'd love to come,' Kate said.

'Really?' Lana let out her held breath.

'But he starts school on Thursday, and the weekends—'

'Tomorrow, then? He could come back with me at lunchtime and I'll have him home whenever you say.'

Kate wondered uneasily how Josh would react to this pressing invitation, but he got on well with Lana and it would give Madge a break.

'Then thank you. I'm sure he'll be delighted,' she said.

CHAPTER 5

Lana Truscott lived in the village of Littlemarsh, off the Shillingham to Broadminster road. The bus ride took half an hour, and it was this that swung the balance in persuading Josh of the desirability of the visit. He had a passion for buses, particularly if he could sit on the top deck.

'It's very kind of Miss Truscott to invite you, and you must behave well and not make too much noise, because her father isn't well.' The child had never seen an invalid and Kate was grateful for Lana's reassurance, which she couldn't have elicited herself.

'I can still go to Tim's in the morning, can't I? We've made a den in a tree and it's the last day we can play there before school.'

The next morning a police constable called at the shop. He looked young and ponderous, reminding Kate irresistibly of Mr Plod in Josh's old colouring book.

'Good morning, madam. New here, aren't you?'

'I started this week. Can I help you?'

'Mr Bailey or Mr Mowbray about?'

'Mr Bailey's on the phone. Can I give him a message?'

'I'll wait till he's free, if that's all right. We're inquiring about any strangers you may have noticed, in connection with the recent murder.'

'There are always strangers. The town's full of tourists all year round.'

'Yes, ma'am, but there are strangers and strangers. The gentlemen will know what we have in mind.' He paused. 'Where do you come from yourself, ma'am?'

'Shillingham.' Kate said briefly.

'Then you'll be aware of the other incident.'

'Of course, by the same man.'

'Too early to say that, ma'am.'

The caution in his voice irritated her. 'But surely—'

Martin's appearance interrupted her, which was probably as well.

'Good morning, Constable, I thought you might be in.'

Kate moved down the shop to deal with a customer and a few minutes later the policeman left.

'A thankless job,' Martin commented when they were alone again, 'flogging round making inquiries. Still, they never know what they might turn up.'

'I hope they find something soon. It's not very pleasant, having a murderer in our midst.'

'He probably isn't, most of the time. He could live anywhere and come here on business. That's what Constable Timms was after. If a particular supplier had been in, and he was also in Shillingham a couple of weeks ago, it could be significant. They'll be inquiring at the bus station and garages, too. Most of the customers there are regulars, and an odd one might stick in the memory.'

As requested, Lana returned Josh at six o'clock. As Kate bathed him, he chatted about the visit.

'We had fish fingers and chips for dinner, 'cos I said I liked them. And there was a cloth on the table with holes all over it. Holes that were *meant* to be there.'

'*Broderie anglaise*, I expect. I hope you didn't spill anything.'

'Only some ketchup, but she said it didn't matter. Then we walked down a long lane to a farm, and there was a baby calf and I was allowed to stroke it, and some piglets and lots of chickens. And when we came back, the boy next door let me hold his rabbit. Then we had tea, with cake and jelly. I haven't had jelly since I was little, but I didn't tell her because she'd made it specially.'

'And how was Mr Truscott? Did he like the fruit?'

'Yes, he said to thank you. He was in bed, and very white, with arms like that.' He made an impossibly small circle with finger and thumb. 'But he laughed a lot and told me stories about when he went to sea.'

'You seem to have had a lovely time. I hope you thanked him properly.'

But having dutifully recounted his doings, Josh's mind had turned to more pressing matters. 'Will you take me to school tomorrow?'

'Of course, since it's your first day. After that, Auntie Madge will wait for us at the corner and take you on with Tim, so I can get back for nine o'clock.'

'Does Daddy know I start tomorrow?'

'Of course he does,' Kate said steadily.

'I can tell him all about it on Saturday.'

Oh God, could he? Would Michael be here on Saturday,

and if so, what mood would he be in? It seemed far longer than four days since she'd seen him.

As they set off for St Benedict's the next morning, Kate's nervousness exceeded her son's. He looked so small in the new uniform, so trustingly confident of holding his own in his new environment, that she felt a lump in her throat. It was with relief that she saw Madge and Tim just ahead of them. Josh shouted, and they waited for them to catch up. The two boys ran on ahead and Madge said quietly, 'Don't worry, Kate, he'll be all right. Paul will keep an eye on him the first few days.'

'But with all this upheaval he mightn't cope as well as he should.'

'He'll be fine, it's you I'm worried about! Look, it's half-day closing isn't it? Come round for the afternoon and I'll invite a few others to meet you.'

'Bless you, Madge,' Kate said gratefully.

But that afternoon, for the first time, she felt an outsider in Madge's house. The other three present were schoolmasters' wives but that was all they had in common. Anne Thompson was young and blushed when spoken to. Her baby, a red-faced nine-month-old, was sleeping in the porch, and Kate had to negotiate his pram in order to get in. Brenda Peters was roughly the same age as herself, a plain but pleasant girl with horn-rimmed spectacles from behind which her large brown eyes looked out in anxious friendliness.

The third member, Sylvia Dane, was older than the others, over forty, Kate hazarded, but her manner was young and she was glossily attractive.

'I believe you work at Pennyfarthings?' she said, as Madge

introduced Kate. 'I'll be sending some of my paintings to your exhibition.'

'Sylvia's an artist,' Madge explained unnecessarily. 'She does wonderful portraits.'

'I'll look forward to seeing them,' Kate murmured.

Madge brought in the tea trolley and for a while the talk was of school matters—new staff, the extended library, a proposed change of uniform. Kate's attention wandered. St Benedict's was so different from the homeliness of Highfield Primary. For the first time she regretted the generosity of Michael's parents, whose educational policy had brought the school within their reach. Suppose Josh were unhappy there? Suppose he wasn't as emotionally secure as she'd assumed? If so, the fault would be hers, for dislodging him at such a crucial time. Suppose—

Her mind skidded back to the present with an uncomfortable jolt as it registered the word 'murder.'

'Sex murderers are all psychopaths,' Sylvia was saying firmly, stirring her tea with a decisive swirling of liquid. 'The lust to kill tied up with the sex urge.'

'There's been no mention of sex,' Brenda objected. 'The women were stabbed, nothing else.'

'Probably impotent, then. But the lipstick's significant, don't you think? Perhaps he's a fetishist of some kind.'

'You're gilding the lily, Sylvia,' Madge admonished, 'and it's bad enough already.'

'Indeed it is. Until they catch him, none of us are safe.' She turned unexpectedly to Kate. 'Especially you, my dear. You're living alone, aren't you, except for your little boy? You mustn't worry, though. We're only just down the road. If you phoned us, Henry could be there in two minutes.'

'Thank you,' said Kate faintly.

Madge changed the conversation and gradually Kate relaxed. It was foolish to identify so strongly with the victims. Despite Sylvia's tactlessness, she was no more at risk than the others.

Paul had been detailed to bring Josh and Tim home, and when they heard his key in the door Kate tensed expectantly. But he came in alone.

'I turned the boys loose in the garden,' he told them. 'They're full of high spirits after being cooped up all day, so I thought they'd better let off some steam.'

'As long as they don't start climbing trees in their new uniform,' Madge said drily.

A thin wail came from the porch as the baby, roused from slumber by the schoolboys, voiced his protest. His mother hurried out to soothe him and the other women also rose to go. Since Paul was home, their own husbands would be on their way.

Kate went to the French windows to call Josh.

'What did you think of Sylvia?' Madge asked, stacking cups and saucers and putting them on the trolley.

'She seemed quite pleasant.'

'But?'

'Perhaps a little overanxious to be one of the girls.'

Madge gave a short laugh. 'In that respect she's ahead of us. Believe it or not, she's the local *femme fatale*. At the moment she's carrying on with someone from school. Everyone knows it, but no one's sure who. The odds-on favourite is Robin Peters.'

'Brenda's husband?'

'Exactly. I was hoping to give her pangs of conscience.'

'But surely he's younger than she is?'

'Of course, a good ten years. It probably restores her

morale, because her husband's quite a bit older. She's always stressing the fact.'

Josh appeared reluctantly at the window, rosy and dishevelled from his chase round the garden, and Kate concluded with gratitude that her concern had been misplaced.

He chattered incessantly all the way home, but though she half-listened, Kate was remembering the talk of murder and, when they reached it, the glass-paned door didn't seem to offer much protection. There was a bolt at the bottom, but it had rusted solid and she was unable to move it. She resolved to have a word with Martin about it in the morning.

The smell of the casserole she'd left in the oven reached them as they went upstairs, and illogically Kate felt better. Somehow, murder and steak and kidney were not of the same world.

Josh ate ravenously. School dinner, she was informed, was 'yuk'—a standard complaint. She didn't doubt he had done it full justice. Meanwhile he bombarded her with a string of surnames, something quite different from his infant days at Highfield. Even Tim had mysteriously metamorphosed into 'Netherby' when spoken of in the context of school.

They watched the statutory hour of television, but by the end of it Josh's eyes were heavy and he didn't make even a token protest at the suggestion of bed. Kate almost wished he had. She would have welcomed his company for a little longer that evening.

Deprived of it, she tidied away the supper things, drew the curtains, and switched on all the lamps. It was an extravagance: she needed only the one by the sofa to read by, but she was not in the mood for shadows. She stood for a moment looking round at the heavy old furniture, the deep chairs, the paintings on the wall. It was a lovely setting but, sadly, it was not home. 'Like living in a museum,' Madge had said, that first day. Completely furnished as it was, there was no scope for personal touches. Apart from her library book on the sofa, the room looked exactly as it had when they arrived. And, she thought suddenly, as it would when they'd gone, completely untouched by their occupancy.

Kate sat down and opened her book, but although she read for some time, she was continually aware of the dark stairwell and the unlit area behind the counter. Eventually, ashamed of herself, she went to put on still more lights.

'Positively no bogeyman!' she said aloud. But her tenuous interest in the book had been broken and, putting it aside, she switched on the television. The newsreader was looking directly at her.

'…and despite intensive searches at the scenes of both crimes, the murder weapon has still not come to light. Anyone—'

Savagely Kate switched channels. It was a very long evening.

Even when, taking her book with her, she went to bed, sleep eluded her. The wind had risen and she lay listening to the rustling of the trees on the Green and the creaking of the old building. Her mind was turning over the events of the day; an invoice she'd mislaid, an indecisive customer, the tea party at Madge's.

'Sex murderers are all psychopaths,' said Sylvia's voice, over and over. Behind her closed lids, Kate saw again details she'd not been aware of at the time: the glistening lipstick (spelling out DELILAH? No—) framing the words above the incongruously poised teacup—psychopath, sex, murder—as though she relished the taste of them.

Unfair! Kate chided herself, opening her eyes. Sylvia had said them only once; it was the obsessive repetition of her own brain that made them obscene. Involuntarily she pictured the stricken women facing their killer, saw the shadowy shape of the murderer, arm raised to plunge the knife home. Psychopath— sex—murder. Had he smacked his lips over the deed as Sylvia so nearly had at the thought of it?

Kate's body was drenched in sweat. She flung the covers off the bed, turned her pillow to the cool side and plumped it into shape. In the next room Josh murmured in his sleep. Kate slid out of bed and padded through to look at him. He too had flung the covers off. One small hand hung over the edge of the bed. Gently she replaced it under the sheet. As she stood looking down at him, the Minster clock chimed four slow quarters, followed by a solitary note. One o'clock. Would she never get to sleep?

Childhood remedies came to mind. A mug of hot milk and a couple of aspirins? It was worth a try. Anything to break the morbid treadmill her brain had embarked on.

She was halfway down the stairs when some slight, indistinct sound brought her to a halt, heart pounding. Control yourself! she thought furiously. Much more of this and she'd really become neurotic. But after another step the sound came again, louder and this time indisputable. Her palms tingled and the couplet flashed through her head: 'By the pricking of my thumbs, Something wicked this way comes.'

Water in the pipes. A mouse. All the explanations Michael had sleepily put forward over the years when, fearful in the dark, she had nudged him to go and investigate. Oh, Michael! God, I wish you were here!

She reached the foot of the stairs and stood stock-still, ears straining. Across the room a chink in the curtains pointed a shaft of moonlight towards her, bleaching the carpet in its path. To the left the flight of stairs led down to the darkness of the passage. Then, as she stood there, with the suddenness of an explosion, light blossomed down below. *Someone had switched on the passage light!*

Scarcely knowing what she did, Kate moved slowly forward until she stood in the middle of the room facing the stairs. No use rushing back to bed. She couldn't hide there not knowing what was below, and there wasn't a lock on Josh's door. It would mean waking him and bundling him into her room, and there wasn't time. All these thoughts cascaded through her mind in a split second, unformed but recognized and accepted. And now there were definite footsteps down there, footsteps that made no attempt to be stealthy, coming closer and closer. If only she'd grabbed something with which to defend herself—the carving knife? No, she thought shudderingly, not the carving knife. No point in making it easy for him. And as the thought crystallized, a man's head and shoulders appeared in the stairwell. Kate froze, waited motionless.

He didn't see her till he reached the top step. Then he stiffened. 'God in heaven!' The words were jolted out of him and at the same moment his hand reached for the switch and the room flooded with harsh light. Kate's eyes hadn't left his face. It changed from a silvery blur to reveal shape and colour, with an expression which must have matched her own. Though she was too terrified to anticipate his words, what he said surprised her.

'Who the bloody hell are you? What are you doing here?'

Kate moistened her lips. 'I think,' she said sharply, 'it is I who should ask you that.' 'Easily answered. This is my flat.'

'Your—' Realization hit her, bringing with it an enervating wave of relief. 'Mr Mowbray?' she whispered incredulously.

'The same.'

'Oh, thank God! I thought you were the murderer!'

'You're too kind.' His voice was brisk, impatient, but as she backed to a chair and lowered herself into it, he said curiously, 'You meant that, didn't you? Why the hell should I be a murderer? And you still haven't said what you're doing here.'

She struggled to collect herself. 'I'm Kate Romilly. I work at the shop.'

'Good God! And Martin let you have the flat? He might have mentioned it, for Pete's sake. He knows I sometimes use it.' He hesitated. 'Look, I'm sorry. It appears neither of us is at fault, and I can see you've had a fright.' She heard amusement creep into his voice. 'Mind you, I'm not denying you frightened the hell out of me, too, standing there white and motionless in the dark like an avenging angel! Are you all right now?'

'I think so.'

He came forward and helped her to her feet and for a moment they stood looking at each other. He was broad-shouldered and rather stocky. His thick straight hair was platinum-blond and the eyes, engaged on their own assessment, a clear hazel, edged with stubby lashes. His mouth quirked suddenly.

'An unconventional meeting, Miss Romilly!'

Belatedly she remembered her thin nightdress and felt the colour come to her face. 'I was going to make a hot drink. I couldn't sleep.'

44

'I don't know about a hot one, but I could use the other kind. Have you anything in the house?'

'Only sherry, I'm afraid.'

'Better than nothing. I suggest then that you point me in its direction while you find yourself a dressing gown, and when we've both recovered our nerve I'll leave you in peace.'

She showed him the cupboard where she'd put the sherry and hurried back upstairs. A quick glance in the mirror confirmed her worst fears. The thin cotton clung to her body like a second skin and her hair was tousled and untidy. Swiftly she brushed it, caught up her dressing gown, thrust her feet into slippers. What a way to meet your new boss! Tomorrow, with Madge, she'd be able to laugh about it.

When she reached the kitchen suitably sheathed, he had two glasses ready.

'Sit down,' he invited. 'You still look shaken. I really am sorry about this.'

'I'm not usually so craven, but everyone's talking about the murders and I couldn't get them out of my head. So naturally, when I heard you coming in...' Her voice trailed helplessly away.

'There was nothing craven in the way you faced me. No hint of turning and running.'

'I couldn't, because of my son.'

His eyes went swiftly to her hand. 'So it's *Mrs* Romilly. I beg your pardon. And you have a child with you?'

'Didn't Martin tell you *anything* about me?'

'Only that he'd found someone at a moment's notice to replace Molly. But admittedly I cut him short. I'd a lot of business to discuss and didn't give it another thought.' He finished his drink and reached out to refill his glass. 'I often bed down here if I'm in the neighbourhood. I've an appointment in the morning, so there was no point in driving all the way to Chipping Claydon.'

'What will you do now? You can't go to an hotel this time of night.'

He smiled slightly. 'It would serve Martin right if I knocked him up. No, I'll sleep in the car. I've done it before.'

Kate took a steadying sip of sherry. 'If you'd be more comfortable on the sofa, you're welcome to stay.' She made an embarrassed little gesture. 'It's your flat, after all.'

'The best offer I've had all week. Sure you wouldn't mind?'

She smiled. 'Not at all. If the murderer does come creeping up, at least he'd find you first!'

'What is all this about a murderer? You're not really expecting one, surely?'

Kate eyed him incredulously. 'Mr Mowbray, I don't know where you've been for the past two weeks, but unless it was Outer Mongolia I can't believe you've not heard of the Delilah murders.'

'Ah! The writing on the mirror? That does ring a bell. Of course, they were in this area, weren't they?' He stood up and stretched. 'If we don't get some sleep, neither of us will be fit for much tomorrow. I've had a long drive and I'm just about dead beat. You go back to bed. I've my night things with me'—he nodded to a valise on the floor—'so I'll just use the bathroom, if I may.'

'I'll say good night, then.'

He raised his glass in a salute and drank from it. But as she reached the stairs his voice stopped her.

'Mrs Romilly?'

'Yes?'

'Might one ask where *Mr* Romilly is?'

'In Shillingham.'

'Ah!'

She waited, but he made no further comment and after a moment she continued up the stairs.

CHAPTER 6

The alarm rang for some time before Kate reached out sleepily to silence it. Then, suddenly wide awake, she sat up. Richard Mowbray was here!

Hastily she pulled on her dressing gown and opened the door. There was no sound of movement from below, and she went quickly into Josh's room. He lay spread-eagled on the bed, warm and tousled like a small animal. Kate gently shook him awake and hurried to the bathroom. The mirror was misted up, the soap wet. Mr Mowbray was ahead of her.

She bathed quickly, supervised the intricacies of Josh's school tie and explained the presence of the visitor downstairs. By the time they went down, Richard Mowbray was draining a mug of coffee.

'I helped myself. Hope you don't mind.' Kate noticed that the hours of sleep had done nothing to lessen his pallor. He shook hands with Josh and put his mug on the table. 'I'll get out of your way, then. Thanks for the accommodation.'

'Won't you have some breakfast?'

'No, thanks, the coffee was fine.' And he was gone, taking his valise with him. Feeling distinctly underslept, Kate set about laying the table.

When she reached the office an hour later, Lana, a faint colour in her cheeks, was opening the mail while Richard Mowbray talked on the telephone. Martin arrived just as he finished.

'Hello there—welcome back. You've met Kate, I take it?'

'Indeed yes. In the middle of the night.'

Though she didn't look up, Lana's fingers paused briefly as Martin, looking from one to the other, exclaimed, 'Oh God! Don't tell me! Didn't I—?'

'No, you bloody didn't!' Richard said amiably. 'I burst into the flat at one a.m. and—Kate—assumed I'd come to cut her throat.'

'I did try to tell you on the phone, but you cut in about the Royal Worcester. So what did you do?'

'It was too late to go elsewhere, so she kindly allowed me use of the sofa. But she'd a nasty few minutes, hearing me crashing up the stairs.'

Martin turned to her and spread his hands. 'What can I say? I'm really very sorry.'

'The bolt on the door is stuck,' Kate said levelly, 'which was why Mr Mowbray was able to get in. Could you have a look at it?'

'So that he can't again?' Martin suggested with a grin. 'Certainly. It probably only needs a spot of oil. Now,'—he turned to Richard—'you'd better fill me in before old Carruthers arrives. How much is this stuff worth?'

'Hell, I was going to entertain him upstairs. We'll have to take him to The George.'

'It's quite tidy up there,' Kate said. 'You're welcome to go up if you'd like to.'

'I think I've imposed enough.'

49

'All the same,' Martin put in, 'it would be far more convenient if Kate doesn't mind. Everything we want to show him is here.'

'Old Carruthers,' an elderly military-looking gentleman, arrived at ten o'clock and the partners duly took him upstairs. Kate could hear them moving about and the low murmur of their voices. At eleven, Lana took up a tray of coffee.

'It must have been a shock,' she commented on her return, 'hearing someone come in the middle of the night.'

Kate sipped her coffee. 'It wasn't too pleasant.'

'How very brave of you to go downstairs.'

'Actually, I *was* downstairs. In the living room, that is. I was about to make myself a drink. But why does Mr Mowbray use the flat? Hasn't he a home of his own?'

'Yes, but it's up on the Gloucestershire borders. In Chipping Claydon.'

'I think he mentioned it. Not very convenient, surely?'

'He spends most of his time travelling to sales and auctions, and he's abroad a lot, so it doesn't make much difference.'

'He's divorced, isn't he?'

'I suppose Mr Bailey told you. It'll be two years ago now.'

'Did you know his wife?'

'She came here once or twice. I didn't care for her.'

'I gather he was pretty upset when she left.'

Lana didn't reply and when Kate glanced at her, she was surprised to see her lip trembling. Could she be nursing a secret passion for Richard Mowbray? After a moment Lana said quietly, 'The end of a marriage is always sad. At least Mr Mow-bray was able to weather it. Other people aren't so strong.'

'You know such people?' probed Kate gently.

'My brother.' The long fingers tightened on the edge of the desk. 'It was a combination of things. He hadn't been well, he was made redundant, then his wife left him.'

'It must have been the last straw. What happened?'

'He—took his own life.' She bent her head.

'Oh, Lana—no! I'm terribly sorry. When did this happen?'

'Six months ago. It nearly killed Father. That's when he took permanently to his bed. Ralph was the apple of his eye, you see.'

'Are there any children?'

Her mouth tightened. 'Yes, Judy. A lovely little girl. Six, she is now—not much younger than your Josh. Since her mother went off without her, Father and I thought we'd be granted custody, but no. *She* came back and claimed her and the court gave in. But a child needs two parents, Mrs Romilly.'

'Yes,' Kate said numbly.

Lana raised her head. 'Forgive me—I've no right to say this— but I'd assumed you were a widow. It was only when Josh came to tea and started chatting about his father that I realized—well—'

'That I'd left him? Nothing's really settled yet. We're just having a cooling-off period.' Why had she said that? Was that really how she regarded it, or was she simply trying to placate Lana, who was clearly upset?

'I hoped it might be that. Josh seems to be expecting his father this weekend.'

'Yes, he'll be down in connection with the murder, anyway.'

'The murder? Your husband's in the police?'

'No, he's editor of the local paper. He—'

'Michael Romilly?' Lana exclaimed, as Martin had before her. 'Of course! Why didn't I make the connection?'

'Probably because you thought I was a widow.'

'Yes, I can see it would be difficult, living up to a man like that.'

Only when Kate thought about it later did that last remark imply she was herself to blame.

Madge telephoned the next morning. 'Sorry to ring you at work, Kate, but Michael's here. Or rather, he's just left on his way to you. I tried to persuade him to wait, but he wasn't in the mood to be reasonable.'

Kate briefly closed her eyes. 'All right, Madge. Thanks for the warning.' She put down the phone and went out into the shop, looking round it like a general sizing up the battlefield. Richard and Martin were out, Lana still closeted in the office. And Josh, when last seen, had been flat on his stomach on the living-room floor, a comic spread out in front of him.

'Of course I'll be all right,' he'd said indignantly as she left him. 'If I want you, I'll come down.'

So she was alone, which was just as well. How much had Madge told him? She had no time to wonder. The door rocked open and Michael, his shoulders wet with rain, came briskly into the shop. He stopped on seeing Kate, and he too glanced quickly round to make sure they were alone.

'So there you are. Have you finished playing games?'

'I'm not playing, Michael. I told you that.'

'I grant you've gone further than I expected. I thought you'd be staying with Madge till I came for you, but she tells me you've not only a job but a flat as well. Isn't that overdoing it?'

'I need both.'

'My dear girl'—she was always his "dear girl" when he was

most annoyed with her—'you know perfectly well you've no intention of carrying this through. When you judge I've pleaded and cajoled enough, you'll come back all right.'

Her head lifted. 'Is that what you're doing, pleading and cajoling? I can't say I noticed.'

His mouth tightened. 'Pack your bags. I'm taking you both home.'

'I'm sorry, Michael, but you're not.'

'Then I'm taking Josh.'

'Wrong again. Josh is at school here. How could you look after him when you work such irregular hours?'

'Damn it, he's my son.'

'You can see him. In fact, he's expecting you. But I advise you not to do anything high-handed like taking him back with you, because then things would get really unpleasant.'

He stood considering, head bent slightly as he weighed the possibilities. It was such a typical stance, so familiar, that Kate's body, not realizing its changed status, gave a little jerk of longing. Michael exuded virility like a male animal, confident and self-aware. No wonder she had rivals.

'As it happens,' he said, coolly looking at her, 'this could be quite convenient. I'll be spending some time here while this murder story holds and I'll need a base.'

'You can't stay here, Michael. I didn't come—'

'Don't be ridiculous, Kate. You're my wife and I have every right to sleep with you.'

Heat flooded over her, and the old treacherous desire. 'It's quite impossible.' She heard her voice rise, but before she could continue the doorbell sounded its warning and Martin came in, pausing as he saw them facing each other.

53

'This is my husband,' Kate said woodenly. 'Martin Bailey, my boss.'

Martin's tone was smooth. 'If you'd like to talk somewhere, I can hold the fort for a while.'

'Thank you.'

Since she'd no wish to parade Michael through the office in front of Lana, Kate went out of the shop door and in the next one. She hadn't looked again at Michael, but he followed her closely. They went in silence up the stairs. Josh was still engrossed in his comic, an open box of crayons beside him.

Kate said with forced brightness, 'Look who's here, darling.'

Josh raised his head, one strand of hair falling over his forehead. 'Hello, Daddy.'

'Hi there.'

No exuberant hugs, no flinging his arms round Michael's knees. He was a very self-contained little boy. Was that her fault? Or should it rather be considered an achievement?

'How's school going down?'

'All right.'

'He's enjoying it very much,' Kate enthused, 'and having Tim with him is a great help.'

'The Netherbys are proving indispensable.'

Josh, opting out of the long words, returned to his comic. Kate said in an undertone, 'Do you want to take him out somewhere?'

'What about you?'

'I work all day Saturday.'

'Well, that's just great, isn't it? When the hell are we going to talk?'

'There's nothing to talk about.'

'Kate, for God's sake!' He paused. 'Please come home.'

'This is home. For the moment, anyway.'

Michael sighed with exasperation. 'All right, we'll postpone our discussion till this evening.' He glanced at his son stretched on the floor. 'What on earth can I do with him all day?'

Kate felt a tinge of sympathy. She didn't doubt Michael was fond of Josh, but he wasn't gifted with patience and found it hard to limit his keen, analytical brain to the compass of his son's understanding.

'Take him to a Chinese restaurant and then to the cinema. By the time that's over I'll be free.'

'Right.' Michael's face mirrored his relief. 'Come on then, Josh. Get your mac and we'll go out for some Chinese.'

'Great!' Josh scrambled happily to his feet and ran up the stairs. His father's eyes followed him.

'How many bedrooms are there?'

'Two.'

'So he's not in with you?'

'No.' She met his eyes steadily. 'And nor will you be.'

He didn't reply. No doubt he felt that after a meal and a bottle of wine—which he'd be sure to bring back—she'd be more accommodating. Josh reappeared fastening his raincoat and the three of them went downstairs and out to the pavement. The rain had almost stopped.

'Family reunion?'

Kate turned to see Richard Mowbray approaching, and perforce introduced him to Michael, who said easily, 'I'll be down here for some days covering the murder. I take it there'd be no objection if I join my family upstairs?'

Richard glanced at Kate, and almost imperceptibly she shook her head.

'Awfully sorry, old man.' His tone was as nonchalant as Michael's. 'Can't be done. There are all kinds of subletting clauses and we have to stick with them. Fire risks and so on.'

'*Fire* risks? But surely—'

'Sorry. Nice to have met you.' And Richard passed into the shop.

Kate avoided her husband's eye. 'See you about five-thirty.' She followed Richard inside and he turned from the vase he was studying.

'Thank you,' she said simply.

'Any time.'

That afternoon was the busiest of the week. Possibly people came in out of the rain, but their shelter proved profitable and the cash register was kept busy. Kate tried to concentrate on her work, but her mind was on the evening ahead. *Children need two parents, Mrs Romilly.*

By the time Michael and Josh returned from the cinema, she had the meal well in hand. She'd reverted to the established Saturday formula: beans on toast for Josh, and when he was in bed, a leisurely meal for herself and Michael. She noted, without comment, that the expected bottle of wine had been placed in the kitchen.

Josh had his meal. Michael bathed him and put him to bed. Routine the same, only the setting different. No, Kate corrected herself, straightening her shoulders. Not only the setting.

By unspoken consent they kept off personal matters as they ate, talking instead of the murders Michael was covering.

'I suppose you didn't know this second woman?' Kate asked him.

'No,' he replied drily. 'It's not only my acquaintances who are murdered.'

'We had a constable round asking questions. He wouldn't even commit himself to its being the same murderer, but surely it must be?'

'God, I hope so! We don't want two nuts rushing about stabbing people and scrawling on mirrors. There must be a connection, if they can spot it. Oddly enough, we reported on the divorce cases of both women.' He smiled mirthlessly. 'Poor Bob got a fair grilling.'

'Who?'

'Bob Preston, who was living with Linda. Prime suspect, of course, most murders being domestic, but luckily for him he was at work at the time, surrounded by people. In any case, if he had done it, you'd think he'd have faked a break-in or robbery or something.'

'Unless he was in a state of shock or being very clever—a double bluff.'

'It wasn't Bob, Kate. Even the police seem satisfied with that. Anyway, he'd no connection with the last one.'

'No *known* connection.'

Michael smiled crookedly. 'You're beginning to sound like my friend Webb.'

'How is the Chief Inspector?'

'Under extreme pressure, especially after the second murder. Fleming's in charge, and he's not one to let the grass grow. He sits in the Incident Room rapping out a constant stream of instructions. He's got them hopping like fleas, according to Dave.' He laid down his knife and fork. 'However, enough of all this. It's time we turned to more personal matters. Do I gather you're really not coming back with me?'

'Not immediately, certainly.'

He lit a cigarette and leant back in his chair, exhaling slowly. 'I seem to have misread the situation. I imagined you'd shot off to Madge's in a fit of pique and I only had to promise to be a good boy for you to come home again.'

'But you've been here during the week, covering the murder. Why didn't you contact me then?'

'I decided to let things ride till the weekend, by which time I thought you'd be ready to see sense. But now that you've found yourself a flat and a job—a new life, in fact—I've had to do some rethinking.'

'Did you reach a conclusion?' Kate's mouth was dry as she waited for his answer.

'Nothing concrete.' He met her eyes through the curling smoke. 'Do you want a divorce?'

'I don't know.'

'Then what's the point of all this?'

Kate drew an unsteady breath. 'It was the only way of showing you how I feel. You wouldn't listen when I tried to explain.'

'So tell me now. How *do* you feel?'

'That if it's to survive, our marriage will have to change drastically.'

'It's no worse than thousands of others. In some respects, a damn sight better.'

'But it wasn't enough, was it?'

'Meaning the "forsaking all others" bit? I admit I've played around. It was nothing serious.'

'It was to me. I was the one sitting at home, waiting and

wondering and having to avoid the pitying looks everyone was giving me. And when you actually refused to support Josh's swim so you could be with that girl—' She choked to a halt.

'Very well, you've made your point. You won't come back but you don't want a divorce, at least not yet. So we'll regard this as a breathing space, a weighing of pros and cons. At the end of six weeks or six months or whatever, you'll have to decide whether or not to come back. And I, whether I'll have you.'

Kate said shakily, 'That sounds fair enough.'

'In the meantime, we're both free agents. We can't reach a decision unless we know how it will be if we plump for divorce. I'll see Josh every weekend, and when we meet we'll behave in a civilized way, no recriminations or hashing over old hurts. Agreed?'

'Agreed,' Kate echoed numbly. It was typical of Michael that he had in a few hours completely adjusted to the situation over which she had agonized for months. It was a challenge, an opening up of new directions, and Michael thrived on both. She suspected that, having accepted the position, he was beginning to enjoy it. But would she?

She said, 'What will you tell everyone? The family, and so on?'

'The truth. That we're going through a sticky patch and decided on a trial separation. Nothing irrevocable, just a waiting period.'

'The family' was all on Michael's side. Kate had been the only child of only children, and both her parents were dead. She'd had no mother to run home to, which, she thought ruefully, was no doubt why she'd turned to Madge.

'In the meantime,' Michael continued, 'I'll speak to Keith about arranging an allowance.'

59

Kate said stiffly, 'There's no need. Your parents' policy covers Josh's fees and I have my salary.'

'There's the rent for this place for a start, and of course you must have maintenance. We'll do things according to the book.'

It was no use arguing once Michael had made up his mind. Ten years of marriage had certainly taught her that. Half an hour later, with everything apparently cut and dried between them, he took his leave. But Kate stood where he had left her for a long time after the sound of his footsteps and the bang of the street door had faded into silence.

CHAPTER 7

Although he wasn't aware of it, Webb followed Michael's car back to Shillingham. It had been an eventful but frustrating week; hours and hours of sifting evidence, comparing statements, checking, questioning, checking again. Two things had developed from the requested phone call to the Assistant Chief Constable. First, as he'd anticipated, the second murder had stepped up official concern and Chief Superintendent Fleming was assigned to the case. Secondly, the centre of operations had been moved from Shillingham to Headquarters at Stonebridge, which was equidistant from both crimes. And, Webb thought wryly, more convenient for the Chief Superintendent.

Not that he had anything against Fleming. He'd have preferred to run the show himself and knew he was capable of it, but higher authority had to be shown in action. And there was grim satisfaction in the fact that, despite the increased backup, Fleming had so far got no further with the second murder than he himself had with the first. The Delilah killer had seemingly appeared out of the blue, made his strike, and disappeared 'leaving no trace behind.'

Not strictly true, of course, Webb conceded, dipping his head-lights for an approaching car. Forensic would certainly dispute it, poring over their infinitesimal samples. But they didn't add up to much. The first victim had some white fibres under her fingernails, most probably from the murderer's gloves. The second only had minute scraps of material from the armchair on which, in her death throes, her fingers had tightened. For the rest, there were no footprints, no conveniently dropped button or hand-kerchief, nothing but a few dried pine-needles trodden into the carpet—and even they hadn't been present at the second crime.

One good thing about Fleming coming in was that, barring fresh developments, he was himself released for what remained of the weekend. 'You look shattered, Dave,' the Chief Superintendent had remarked. 'Better knock off till Monday and come back to it fresh. We'll contact you if we need you.'

He'd hardly been in the flat all week, reaching it at varying hours of the late evening or early morning only to fall into exhausted sleep. Now, with a few hours in hand, he'd better make his peace with Hannah. Hell, it was almost like being married again.

On an impulse he stopped at a roadside flower stall and bought a bunch of dahlias, spiky and wet with the day's rain. They might ease the way. But dammit, she'd had no right to assume he'd spend his birthday with her. He'd been looking forward to a day alone sketching and painting; how should he know she was preparing a special meal?

All the same, he could at least have returned to eat it with her, instead of spending the evening at the pub. That had been sheer bloody-mindedness.

The sun was setting as he turned into Hillcrest and the purple clouds were tinged with gold. A hundred years ago, this had been a well-to-do avenue of stately, well-spaced houses in their own grounds. But the zealous bulldozers of the fifties had razed all but a few and in their place, like a flock of gawky phoenixes, had arisen one block after another of slab-faced flats, each pretentiously called after the dignified old house it replaced.

Webb turned into the driveway of Beechcroft Mansions and garaged his car for the first time in a week. Hannah's flat on the first floor, more spacious than his, looked out over the large back gardens, well-tended now by contract gardeners and divided equally between the six flats in the block. He had never made use of his own portion.

He paused, pocketing the garage key, and let his eyes pass over the sweeping lawn, the vivid flower beds and the wild area at the far end. If he'd had his sketch-pad handy he might have been tempted to capture that interplay of light and shade as evening shadows advanced across the grass.

With a mental shrug he turned away, walked back round the house and in the front door. Usually he went up the stairs two at a time but it was a measure of his tiredness that he opted this evening for the lift, sailing without effort to the second floor, the bunch of dahlias in one hand, his meagre supper in the other. He let himself into the flat and on impulse crossed to the window and stood looking out. No, he didn't envy Hannah her view of trees and garden. From his eyrie up here he looked right down the hill to Shillingham nestling at the foot, lights twinkling now at the approach of darkness. His patch, he thought, his little kingdom.

God, he was more tired than he'd thought! He turned away with a twisted smile, mocking his moment of sentiment. All the same, he liked his home, the position of it high on the hill, the neat masculinity of the interior.

In the pocket-sized kitchen he dumped the flowers on the draining board and unwrapped the solitary pork chop, deciding to make some chips to go with it. When his marriage broke up three years previously, he'd promised himself grimly that he wouldn't live out of tins, and it was characteristic of him that, having made the decision, there was no tin-opener in the flat. Methodically he tied an apron round his middle and began to peel potatoes. He didn't regret his aloneness. There was no longer any need to make phone calls of apology if he was late or called away, no one to whom he was accountable, and there was a certain bleak freedom in that. Which, he thought solemnly, brought him back to Hannah.

It wasn't that she made claims on him—he couldn't accuse her of that—but, circumstances being what they were, he couldn't escape a sense of indebtedness.

An hour later, having eaten and tidied everything away, Webb collected the flowers, their purple heads already wilting in their paper sheath, and, pulling his door shut behind him, ran lightly down the stairs to ring Hannah's bell.

It was some moments before she came to the door, wearing a housecoat and with a towel swathed round her head.

'Hello, David. Come in. I'm just washing my hair.' No hint in her voice of sulking or reproach, either for the circumstances of their last encounter or of the week's silence that had followed it. But nor should there be, he reminded himself, following her inside.

'I presume you're not on duty, so pour yourself a drink. I'll be with you in a moment.'

She disappeared and Webb went into the sitting room. This flat was a different layout from his, larger, more airy, and stamped with an indefinable character as charming and elusive as Hannah herself. There were watercolours on the walls, chairs in apple-green velvet, and the windows were open to the dark garden below. Though she hadn't noticed his flowers, there were plenty of others, crammed into vases and containers round the room and all managing to look as though they'd been professionally arranged.

Hannah came back, her hair, towel-dry, about her shoulders. 'Are those flowers for me? How lovely—thank you.'

They were the first he'd bought her and he was relieved that she treated them so naturally. He watched as she bent to take a vase from a low cupboard, and it wasn't only the artist in him that appreciated the curve of her body. Who was he fooling? He knew damn well why he was here, and it had precious little to do with apologizing. Despite himself, he said baldly, 'I use you. You know that, don't you?'

She turned from arranging the shaggy heads, momentarily surprised. 'And I you. It works both ways.'

'I wasn't at all sure I'd be welcome.'

'Hence the peace offering?' She smiled in genuine amusement.

'I *am* sorry, Hannah. About last weekend. It was thoughtless of me—'

'No,' she interrupted swiftly. 'It was my fault for keeping the dinner a surprise. It never occurred to me you might have other plans, and that was stupid.'

'I could have changed them.' He was his own prosecuting counsel.

'But why should you? It was your birthday.' And she his

65

defence. Dismissing the conversation, she ran her fingers through her thick hair to dry it. 'I don't see that drink.'

'I hadn't got round to pouring it.'

'Do it now, then, and one for me, too.'

She moved to the windows and closed them. 'It's getting cooler in the evenings, have you noticed? Or perhaps it's just my wet hair. I'll put the gas fire on to dry it, so take off your jacket if you like.'

There were no overhead lights and the lamp in the corner shed only a soft, localized gleam. Webb poured out two glasses, went through to the fridge for ice. Even the kitchen blossomed under Hannah's touch. There were more flowers on the windowsill, in pots this time. A selection of exotic postcards was pinned to a notice board and the air smelled of spices.

When he returned she was kneeling by the gas fire, her hair reflecting the redness of the element, her neck fragile and exposed. He had an overpowering desire to bend and kiss it. Instead, he said more brusquely than he'd intended, 'Your drink.'

'Thanks. Put it on the table, will you?'

He lowered himself into a button-backed chair beside her, his eyes still on her shining hair.

'I presume you've had a bad week,' she went on quietly. 'I read about the other murder.'

'It's been tiring, I'll say that.'

'Any progress?'

'Not that you'd notice.'

'Poor David. I've been thinking about you.'

'And what have you been doing? Didn't school start this week?'

'Yes, Thursday. Back in the old routine.'

He smiled suddenly. 'Looking at you now, I can think of no one less like a deputy headmistress!'

She laughed in her throat and he felt his pulses quicken. 'Hannah—' He broke off, not knowing what he wanted to say. She turned her head under the curtain of hair and then, shaking it back, swivelled round to look at him. She was lovely, he thought, with her wide brow and clear grey eyes that met his so steadily. His gaze moved across her face, the high cheekbones, soft, generous mouth and, on either side, the curtain of thick tawny hair, with the gold highlights still lingering from the summer sun. Their eyes locked and she rose slowly to her feet.

'I think, Chief Inspector, that you'd better put that glass down before you spill it.'

On the way through to the bedroom, she asked suddenly, 'Suppose they need to contact you?' and saw that she'd embarrassed him. He met her eyes, smiled slightly, and looked away.

'I gave them this number,' he admitted.

So! she thought, and was satisfied.

Much later, as an owl swooped over the garden with its haunting cry, only Hannah heard it. Beside her, David Webb slept the sleep of exhaustion. She turned her head but in the pale moonlight could only distinguish the outline of his head, a darkness in the indented pillow.

It was an odd relationship, hers and David's. They had met a year ago, when a spate of anonymous letters among the staff had led Gwen to call in the police. Now, lying in the luminous darkness, Hannah tried to remember her first impression of him. He wasn't a handsome man. In repose his face had a stern, unhappy look, bitterness about the mouth and disillusion in the eyes. Yet his smile had a charm which constantly surprised those who saw it for the first time. It was probably the smile that started it, warming her to the reserved man behind it, with his quiet manners and the soft hint of Broadshire in his voice.

As she came to know him better, she found him a man of contradictions: ruthless yet compassionate; shrewd, but capable of surprising naivety, hard-headed yet with an artistic gift that produced pleasing landscapes as well as startlingly life-like caricatures. Even their relationship was two-sided: contented, undemanding friendship for long weeks and urgent comings together like tonight.

It was she who had told him of the vacant flat upstairs. At the time they met, David was still in the lodgings to which he'd moved when his wife left. Hearing that he wanted somewhere of his own, small and easily managed, Beechcroft had seemed the perfect solution. Even so, Hannah had weighed the position carefully before mentioning it. His moving into the same building would inevitably draw them closer, and she had no wish to embark on a relationship which might make claims on her. That David apparently felt the same was an enormous relief, and ironically enough their first love-making had been at her instigation.

Nostalgically, Hannah thought back to it. It had happened soon after David moved in, when he was working on a child-murder case. It was obvious that he was deeply disturbed by it, but though they'd sat for hours drinking coffee he'd avoided all mention of the case and she hadn't liked to raise the subject. Then, when he looked at the clock and rose reluctantly to his feet, she had said quite spontaneously, 'I don't think you should be alone tonight.' It had been as simple as that.

And, after their love-making, he had suddenly started to talk. It had all come pouring out till she had to bite her lip to prevent herself crying out for him to stop. And that proved the forerunner of other occasions. The only time he spoke of things that mattered to him was in bed. Their physical intimacy seemed to trigger a corresponding mental one and he would settle back with an arm behind his head and begin to talk, quietly and steadily, to himself, she sometimes felt, as much as to her, using her as a sounding board for his theories and beliefs. She would listen drowsily, aware that the only contribution required of her was her presence, and occasionally, guiltily, fall briefly asleep, to wake minutes later to the steady rhythm of his voice.

It had been the same tonight: his doubts and worries about the Delilah killings, his fear that the murderer would strike again before they could find him.

Yes, all in all it was an unusual relationship, but one that she treasured and which suited them both very well. She stretched sleepily, feeling the cool sheet move over her naked body. Beside her David stirred and sighed in his sleep. Hannah leaned over and gently kissed the hump of his bare shoulder. Then, snuggling down beside him, she fell asleep.

CHAPTER 8

Madge had warned Kate that as a school chorister Josh would be expected to attend services in the Minster. 'On the third Sunday every month they join the main choir for ten o'clock matins. It's very impressive, Kate. They wear cassocks and white ruffs and look quite angelic! On the other Sundays, like tomorrow, there's school evensong at six-thirty—the public go at four o'clock. Paul and I'll call for you and we can go together.'

It was the first time Kate had been inside the Minster and its sheer size overpowered her. The soaring arches, the richness of stained glass, the cold, rounded marble effigies filled her with a sense of awe, bearing witness as they did to a daily round of worship stretching back seven hundred years. She was proud that her son now played a part in its continuance.

On the Monday morning, it was a surprise to find Richard Mowbray in the shop. 'I thought you'd have been off on your travels again by now,' Kate told him.

'I'll be here for a while yet. We've an art exhibition coming off shortly and there's a lot of arranging to do.'

'And you'd been expecting to stay at the flat? I'm so sorry. You're surely not going home every night?'

'No, Martin and Nella are putting me up. They insist it doesn't put them out, and I'm inclined to believe them. By the way, you'll be glad to hear you have Nella's seal of approval.'

'I'm very relieved.'

He flicked through some brochures, not looking at her. 'Weekend all right?'

'We survived.'

When Lana came in, she was paler than ever and her skin had a glistening sheen. Kate watched her through the window as she made her daily trip to the bird table, saw her sway and wipe the back of her hand across her forehead.

'You don't look well, Lana,' she said with concern as the woman came back into the office. 'Surely you shouldn't have come in this morning?'

'I'm all right.' Lana's shallow, rapid breathing belied her words. 'I've a sore throat, but it'll pass. I can't afford to be ill.' She took the cover off her machine and sat down. 'Did you have a good weekend?'

'So-so.'

'Your husband came, I gather.'

'Oh yes.'

'I'm so glad.'

Richard came in with a list in his hand. 'Publicity all in hand for the exhibition, Lana? Posters up, and so on?'

'Yes, Mr Mowbray. The leaflets are going out with newspaper deliveries this week and I've arranged for a write-up in the *Evening News*.'

'Fine. Then all we do now is pray for good weather.' He turned to Kate. 'We serve wine in the courtyard the first evening, with a few paintings tastefully arranged, though of course the main exhibition is inside.'

'When does it take place?'

'The private view's a week on Wednesday, then the paintings are on show for ten days. Would you be available to help out that Wednesday? Serve the drinks and generally look decorative?'

'I should think so.' Kate saw that Lana's face, bent ostentatiously over her papers, had turned a dull brick red. 'Doesn't Lana—?'

'She can't leave her father in the evenings.'

Lana looked up, her eyes fixed on a patch of wall between them. 'As you know,' she said tightly, 'I can always arrange to be available if I'm needed, but I shouldn't of course fill the requirement of looking decorative.'

'Lana, my love, you're completely indispensable, as well you know, but you're the first to admit you hate mixing with people. Be thankful you're not called on to socialize.'

Martin, who had appeared in the doorway during the exchange, caught Kate's eye and winked at her. It appeared Lana's weakness for Richard was no secret. Kate felt a wave of protectiveness towards her, combined with rather angry sympathy. When the men had gone, she said lightly, 'You get out in the evenings sometimes, then?'

Lana nodded, still embarrassed and resentful, but a moment later added, 'Actually, I have every Thursday free. Father has a friend in the next village who comes once a week to play chess. I cook them an evening meal, then I'm free till about eleven.'

'You must come over for supper sometime.'

'That's very kind. I should enjoy it.' Her smile ended in a wince of pain and she put a hand to her head.

'You're no better, are you?'

'It's only a headache.'

Lana was still protesting her fitness the next morning, by which time it was clear she was really ill. But as Kate's anxious inquiries were cut short, she had to accept there was nothing she could do.

Thoughts of Lana were banished from her head that lunchtime by an unexpected meeting with Michael. He came hurrying down the steps of the bank as she was passing.

'Hello,' Kate said, feeling foolish.

'On your way to lunch? I'll join you.'

Her eyes widened and he added softly, 'Civilized behaviour, remember. Nothing compromising about lunch.' He took her by the arm and led her down the High Street to the nearest pub. It was very crowded but they managed to find a corner table.

'You're still on the murder?' Kate asked. 'Isn't Bill getting restive?'

Bill Hardy was the reporter into whose hands murder cases usually fell.

'He came down with me, but he knows every so often I get my teeth into a story and like to see it through. Also, the Big White Chief wants me to do what he calls an investigative feature on the murders instead of my Saturday column, which gives me a bit more leeway. There was some excitement yesterday when the police thought they'd found the murder weapon, but now they're not so sure.'

'Where was it?'

'On waste ground behind the market. It had stains which

could have been blood, but there's some doubt that the blade was the right shape to have inflicted the wounds.' He paused. 'There are several letters for you at home. I'll bring them when I collect Josh.'

Kate's mind was still on the weapon. 'Was the same knife used in both cases?'

'It left the same type of wound.'

'Then if he did throw it away, perhaps he doesn't intend to commit any more murders.'

'I doubt if we've seen the end of them yet.'

'Why?'

'Because by now he'll be enjoying the publicity. He deliberately draws attention to himself with his Delilah trademark, and Webb reckons his ego's building up all the time. If he enjoys reading about himself, he won't want the interest to die down, and one way to keep it going is to commit another murder.'

'Just to stay in the headlines?' Kate stared at him in horror.

'Oh, I daresay he's got some complex about women, which was what started him off in the first place. But if he's led an uninteresting life and no one's ever taken much notice of him, you can understand how he'd become hooked on the notoriety.'

'A psychopath?' Kate asked fearfully, remembering Sylvia.

'Almost certainly.' Michael unconcernedly continued with his lunch, but Kate's appetite was gone.

'Do the police think there'll be another murder?' she persisted.

'If they don't catch him first.' He glanced across at her. 'You're not usually so interested in murder cases.'

It was true. But as she'd already discovered, the Delilah murders held a morbid fascination for her, a sense of personal involvement, even personal threat, which no amount of logic could dispel.

'No point in worrying,' he added when she didn't speak. 'Murders have been with us since Cain and Abel and will be as long again.'

Kate said with an effort, 'Do they think he knew both women?'

'Must have done. The last one was highly respectable and not given to taking strange men into her home.'

'So if they can find a common link—'

'Quite,' said Michael drily. 'Simple, isn't it?'

It was no surprise the following morning when Lana phoned to say she wouldn't be in.

'About time!' Kate said severely. 'Don't worry about anything, I can cope. Phone the doctor and go back to bed.'

'But what about Father?'

'Surely one of the neighbours could—'

'I feel faint,' Lana interrupted urgently, 'I'll have to hang up. I'll be back as soon as I can.'

Kate worried about Lana all morning and at lunchtime, reaching a decision, she phoned Madge.

'Could you be an angel and keep Josh this afternoon till I collect him? Lana Truscott's not well and apparently there's no one to look after either her or her father. I thought I'd go over for a couple of hours and make myself useful, since it's half-day closing.'

'No problem. Stay for supper if you like; you won't have time to prepare anything.'

'Thanks, Madge.'

Having checked Lana's address from the filing cabinet, Kate bought a few provisions and collected her car from Lady Ann Square. She hadn't used it during the ten days she'd been in Broadminster and the engine was slow to start.

It was a pleasant day for a drive. The morning mist had given way to thick sunshine, which lay like a benediction on the autumn fields. Overhead against the blue arch of the sky a hawk hung like a chainless pendant before dropping silently on its prey.

Kate turned off the main road at the Littlemarsh sign, hoping apprehensively that her visit would not be taken as interference. She hadn't realized how small the village was. There seemed to be only the one road, with a few cottages on either side. Behind them, fields stretched to the skyline, some full of crops, some grazing land for cattle. The only address she had was The White Cottage, and Kate slowed down, eyes scanning both sides of the road. She passed several farms, a church, and a general store, and was beginning to think she must have missed the Truscotts' house when, almost at the end of the village, she came to it.

With a sigh of relief she parked the car, collected her purchases and walked up the path. The small garden was tidy and colourful in a regimented fashion, as though each flower knew better than to bloom out of place. The white step gleamed, the paint-work was clean and new. Kate raised the brass knocker and let it fall. Hardly surprisingly, no one came to answer it. Experimentally she turned the handle and the door swung open. The little hallway was deserted and there was a lingering smell of furniture polish. An old-fashioned coat-stand stood on the right; Kate recognized Lana's jacket among the others. From a window on the landing the sunshine streamed down the blue-carpeted stairs as though inviting her to climb them.

'Lana?' she called softly. 'It's Kate. Can I come up?'

There was no reply. A quick glance through the open doors

beside her showed the rooms to be empty. Kate went up the stairs, calling as she went. 'It's Kate, Lana. Are you there?'

Still no answer, and now the silence took on an eerie quality. Kate ran up the last few steps and pushed open the first door she came to. Lana was lying on her back, her face as white as the pillow and her dark hair spread loose about her. So still was she that for a heart-stopping moment Kate doubted if she were alive. Then her eyes opened, she gave a gasp and struggled into a sitting position.

Kate said contritely, 'I didn't mean to startle you. I knocked, but the door was on the latch.'

'I left it for the doctor.' Lana was staring at her with an incomprehension left from sleep. 'What are you doing here? Is something wrong?'

'No, no, I thought you might need help. You said there wasn't anyone else.'

Lana flushed. 'That's very kind. The neighbours would come if I asked them, but I prefer to keep to myself. Ralph always said I was too independent for my own good.'

'Well, now I'm here I'm going to cook lunch. I bought some fish—it doesn't take much eating.'

'Oh, Mrs Romilly!' For a startled moment Kate thought she was about to weep.

'I do wish you'd call me Kate,' she said.

'Thank you, yes. I—it's just that I'm not used to being looked after. I'll come down and show you where everything is.'

'Indeed you won't. I'm quite capable of finding what I need.'

Cutting off further protests, Kate returned downstairs. The kitchen was at the back of the hall and its window looked out onto a small garden. The lawn was square and neatly cut, edged with flower beds as geometrically trimmed as at the front. The shed was freshly creosoted and a little gate in the back fence gave access to a wood behind. It was all immaculate but at the same time anonymous, with no hint of love having gone into the planning of it. Rent-a-Garden, Kate thought facetiously.

And she realized that the house itself bore the same lack of personality. All was tidy but there were no spontaneous touches to give a clue to the personality of those who lived here, no scrawled shopping list or rescued daisies in a jar, no gardening shoes behind the door. There was a disquieting sensation of having stepped back in time to the nineteen-thirties and Kate saw that the kitchen was much as it must have been then. There was no fridge or washing machine and the gas cooker was a model long discontinued. A box of Swan Vesta matches stood beside it.

In her search for milk and butter she located the larder, complete with stone slab and ancient meat safe. A row of old-fashioned sweet jars were ranged along the floor, containing, according to their labels, an assortment of pickles and chutneys. Kate, guiltily thinking of her trips to the supermarket, felt increasingly inadequate.

The other necessities were readily to hand, though her search for trays took several minutes, involving the fruitless opening of several cupboards. She even looked under the stairs, but all that was revealed was a carpet sweeper, some cleaning equipment, and a crash helmet, evidently belonging to Lana's dead brother. Kate was on the point of calling upstairs when she discovered the trays neatly slotted in a space behind the door.

She laid them as attractively as possible and cast a critical eye over the plates: crisp fish, creamed potatoes, parsley sauce. It was the best she could do with the ingredients to hand.

By the time she returned upstairs Lana had woken her father and propped him up in bed. He greeted Kate with a smile. 'Lana tells me how kind you're being. We're most grateful. Without Lana here our little world grinds to a halt, Mrs Romilly. Not,' he added with a rueful smile, 'that mine revolves all that quickly at the best of times. You know, I resolved when I took permanently to my bed that I'd take the chance to enrich my mind: read all the classics I'd never had time for, and so on. But to my chagrin all I seem to do is sleep—a quite unbelievable amount. I'm ashamed sometimes, when Lana wakes me for a meal and I find how many hours have been wasted.'

The three of them lunched together in Mr Truscott's room, Kate on a bedroom chair, Lana on a stool. Most of the talk was of Josh, who had made an impression on the old man. 'Such a bright boy,' he said more than once. 'He reminds me of my son at the same age.'

Kate was relieved that both invalids finished their meal, Lana eating daintily in a succession of small, quick forkfuls like one of the birds at her seed tray, her father more slowly as though the effort tired him, the knife and fork heavy in his hands.

After the meal, brushing away their protests, she washed up and cleared away, freshened both bedrooms, and gave the rooms downstairs a quick dust. Before she left, she inquired if there were any provisions they needed. 'I can easily call at the village shop and slip back with something.'

'No, no, I'll be better tomorrow,' Lana assured her.

'Don't come to work till Monday, will you, or you'll make yourself ill again.'

'We'll see, but in the meantime we won't starve.' She flushed. 'That sounds ungracious. It's very, very kind of you to put yourself out like this, Mrs—Kate. We do appreciate it and Father so enjoyed meeting you. He doesn't see many people.'

Kate nearly pointed out that if his daughter weren't so set against visitors he would see more, but she wisely kept silent. Lana was obviously devoted to the old man and did her best for him according to her lights. Her reserve was by now so much a part of her, she was no doubt incapable of overcoming it.

That evening, relaxed in front of a log fire, for it had turned cool, Kate related her thoughts to Paul and Madge. 'She misses so much, that's the tragedy, and so does her father. If only she could relax and be more forthcoming, people would meet her halfway, but they think she's standoffish. It's a shame, because really she's just painfully shy.'

'Molly didn't put it so kindly,' Madge remembered with a smile. 'She referred to her as a repressed spinster!'

'Well, she's certainly carrying a torch for Richard. It's touching, really. She blushes like a schoolgirl every time he appears.'

'All dream stuff,' Paul said with male scepticism. 'In the unlikely event of his making a pass at her, she'd probably have hysterics. A knight errant is only acceptable as long as he stays safely on his charger.'

Whether because of Kate's advice or her own weakness, Lana did not appear again that week and Kate was extremely busy. There were last-minute arrangements about the exhibition, correspondence to deal with, and the shop itself to be attended. Fortunately both partners were in evidence and Martin helped out with the customers while Richard instructed Kate in the mysteries of the filing cabinet.

On the Saturday morning, Josh came downstairs to await collection by his father, sitting contentedly drawing at the other side of the desk.

'Have you the list of paintings handy?' Richard asked Kate. 'I want to check how many Daniel Plumb's submitting this year. He's always a big draw.'

'I think it's here.' Kate leafed through the papers on Lana's desk.

'That's it. Good.' He bent over her, his finger running down the sheet of paper, and she watched its progress. It was stubby and covered with pale hair, the nail short and rounded. She was aware of the singularly antiseptic smell of him, composed of carbolic soap with a faint underlying hint of tobacco. Kate guessed there would be no after-shave in his bathroom cabinet. It occurred to her quite suddenly that it was unlikely he had been celibate during the two years since his divorce, and with a slight sense of shock discovered that she found him attractive. It was the first time she had stood outside the confines of her allegiance to Michael, and the sensation was not comfortable.

'Good morning.'

All three of them looked up to see Michael himself standing in the doorway. Richard straightened slowly and for a moment the two men's gaze held. Then Josh slid off his chair.

'Look what I've drawn, Daddy.'

'That's very good,' Michael said, but his eyes were on Kate. Almost, she wondered, as if he'd read her mind in that moment before she was aware of his presence. 'I'll bring him back at six,' he added abruptly, and it was only when he and Josh had gone that Kate realized she hadn't spoken a word to him. She looked up at Richard, to find his eyes consideringly on her.

'Should I have been tactful and left you alone? It happened so quickly.'

'The time for tact has passed,' she replied.

'Oh?'

'We've decided on a trial separation, to see how things go.'

'I see.' Apparently losing interest, he glanced down again at the list of paintings. 'By the way, it occurred to me that Wednesday evening might be disturbing for Josh. Would it be an idea for him to spend the night with your friend?'

'Perhaps it would, yes. He could go to school with Tim the next morning. Thank you for thinking of it.'

Kate wondered uneasily if Michael would again expect a meal when he returned Josh that evening. Did this, like the pub lunch, come within the confines of civilized behaviour? She hoped not but allowed enough food to cover the eventuality. However, when at six o'clock the doorbell rang and she went downstairs, it was to see Josh's face peering through the glass. He was alone. As Kate opened the door a car engine started up and Michael, who had waited till she admitted the child, drove away with a briefly raised hand.

'I wondered if Daddy would be staying for supper,' she said as they went back upstairs.

'He's going out with friends.'

Plural? Kate wondered, or was that for Josh's benefit? But Michael had warned her that for the moment they were free agents.

CHAPTER 9

On the Monday, Lana was back at her desk, her habitual pallor giving no indication of the extent of her recovery. But she assured everyone she was completely well again, apologized for her absence, and promptly buried herself in the pile of work which Kate had not had time to go through.

During Tuesday, the paintings for the exhibition began to arrive. The storeroom had been tidied to receive them and Kate, Richard, and Lana worked continuously, numbering the frames, stacking them against the wall, and checking them on the list. Kate was interested to see Sylvia Dane's exhibits, and to her surprise found they were brilliant. She had the true artist's ability to look beyond the planes of the face, the veiled wariness of the eyes, to a deeper understanding of the personality beneath, ignoring, sometimes ruthlessly, the inept façade the sitter had erected to preserve his privacy. If these were not portraits to appeal to the vain and self-satisfied, nor were they uncompromisingly 'warts and all.' For combined with their truthfulness an abrasive kindliness showed through as though, having stripped away the surface pretence, the artist was saying, 'There's no need to hide. You can face yourself now.'

Kate walked along the row of pictures studying each one: a young man, sensitive, touchingly unsure of himself; a child, laughing out of the frame; an old man, lined and weathered with the toll of the years; a dreaming girl. She felt embarrassed to meet the painted eyes while their inner beings were thus exposed to view.

'Fantastic, aren't they?' Richard commented. 'You feel you know the sitter personally. She's one of the country's leading portrait painters but the society crowd daren't go near her!'

Kate understood what he meant.

That afternoon, Constable Timms put in another appearance. 'We'd be grateful, sir, if you'd keep an eye open while this exhibition's on. There have been antique knockers in the area from time to time, and this could tie in with our inquiries.'

'We'll keep our eyes peeled,' Martin promised, 'but we expect a crowd and it won't be easy to spot strangers.'

When they closed on Wednesday, they had two hours in which to set up everything, and Kate at last appreciated the work Richard and Lana had done, deciding in advance where each painting should be placed.

'It's going to be a fine evening,' Martin said with satisfaction. 'We can start setting up things in the courtyard.' Between them they wiped the wrought-iron tables and pushed them back against the walls. There was enough space for some dozen canvases outside.

'Doesn't the gallery along the road resent the competition?' Kate asked.

'Not at all.' Richard stood back to study the effect. 'It's *quid pro quo.* Anything that stimulates an interest in art can only benefit them. People often go straight on from here.'

By six-thirty everything was ready. The men went home to change and Kate returned to the flat. It seemed quiet without Josh. She bathed quickly and washed her hair, then selected a demure long-sleeved dress in rose lace which she had worn to Press Club dinners with Michael.

The next few hours passed quickly. The shop was crowded by an eager, appreciative throng, all exclaiming at the paintings, studying their catalogues, and gratefully accepting the glasses of wine which Kate offered them. Was there a murderer among them? She dismissed the idea as absurd.

Martin was in the courtyard with Nella, who, in purple dress and emerald scarf, was more exotic than any of the artists. For the most part, the latter were men with beards and little women in hats, but when Kate tried to match artist with picture, she was continually surprised. A large, clumsy-looking man had executed an exquisite floral painting, an elderly lady a strident jungle scene.

Someone touched her arm and she turned to see Sylvia Dane, flushed and animated, a grey-haired man at her side.

'Good evening, Kate. This seems a very successful gathering. May I introduce my husband, Henry?'

He came forward, quiet, bespectacled, with a gentle smile. 'How do you do, Mrs Romilly. I believe I've the pleasure of taking your son for mathematics.'

'I'm glad it's a pleasure!' Kate smiled, and turned to Sylvia. 'Madge was right, your portraits are wonderful. That one of the old man particularly.'

'Oh yes, old Mr Bennett.' Sylvia looked pleased.

'How many sittings do you need for something like that?'

'It's pretty flexible, really. Many of the people I paint can't spare the time to sit around for hours on end. I've developed the technique of making lots of lightning sketches from all angles, catching fleeting expressions and so on. Then I decide on the position of the sitter, sketch that, and beaver away by myself, with just occasional "refresher" studies. It works particularly well with children, who won't sit still anyway.'

Darkness fell, a breeze sprang up, and they moved back indoors. Several paintings already bore a satisfying red dot denoting a sale. Everyone seemed well pleased with the evening, and by nine-thirty all the guests had gone.

Kate collected the empty glasses.

'Put them back in their box,' Martin told her. 'We'll take them home and wash them in the machine. Now, who's hungry?'

'We always go for a meal after the view,' Richard explained. 'Another reason for proposing Josh's absence! The usual choice is The Duck Press on the Heatherton Road. Do you know it?'

Kate shook her head.

'I'll bring the car round,' Richard added, 'while the rest of you lock up.'

The drive took only twenty minutes. The restaurant was a cleverly converted barn, made up of a series of low-beamed rooms leading off one another. There was an air of quiet, unobtrusive luxury and Kate settled back to enjoy herself. It was a long time since she'd been out for dinner.

'Choose what you like, it's all on expenses,' Martin told her. 'We've earned it, after all the work we've put in. Except Nella, of course. She's just along for the ride.'

'Lana deserves this more than I do,' Kate remarked. 'She

was saying she's been working towards the exhibition for the last six months.'

'Can you imagine Lana in this setting?' Richard asked with a short laugh. And, looking at the dim lights, the suave, silent waiters and thick napery, Kate thought back to the impersonal house at Littlemarsh and felt a touch of sadness.

'What's the latest on the murders, Kate?' Martin asked suddenly.

'How on earth should Kate know?' Nella demanded.

'Didn't I tell you, her husband's editor of the local rag. He has a cosy relationship with the fuzz.'

Nella gave a mock shudder. 'All I can say is, I'm glad I'm not divorced. I should hate to have my lipstick on a mirror.'

Richard poured out the wine. 'Thousands of women are divorced these days. It could just be coincidence.'

'But the word "Delilah,"' Martin protested. 'Surely that implies censure, accusation? I'd say the police should be looking for a deserted husband out for revenge.' There was a brittle silence, then he gave a nervous laugh. 'Present company excepted, of course! Sorry, Richard.'

Richard did not, as Kate expected, laugh the remark off. He gave no indication of having heard it, and a moment later Martin went on, 'I'm probably way off-beam. It's just how it struck me, that's all.'

Kate had noticed before that Martin, the junior partner, was sometimes less than at ease in Richard's company, and wondered what had brought them together.

Nella, of course, had no reservations and as always spoke frankly. 'But if it was a deserted husband, wouldn't he rape the victims before killing them? Or does he get his kicks in other ways? The lipstick could be a phallic symbol, I suppose.'

Richard said caustically, 'You're very quiet, Kate. No interesting theories to put forward?'

'I'm afraid not. I enjoy murder between the pages of a book, but these are a bit too close to home.'

'Of course, your husband knew Number One, didn't he?' Martin cut in. 'I suppose it follows he could also know the murderer.'

'Or *be* the murderer!' Nella said, and grinned broadly. 'And *I* didn't mean *that*, either!'

With an uncomfortable glance at Richard, Martin changed the subject and there was no more talk of murder.

Martin and Nella spent the return journey entwined on the back seat of the car.

'Love's young dream!' Richard said cynically in a low voice. 'We could tell them a thing or two, couldn't we?'

Kate didn't reply but tears stung her eyes as memories rushed back of happier days: the expression on Michael's face when he first saw Josh, the bunches of flowers which had not been forthcoming for a very long time. Were Martin and Nella right to keep an escape clause in their relationship? Would they really, when the time came, be able to leave each other without a backward glance? Or would this early freedom condition them for a more permanent relationship in the future, more securely based than either Richard's marriage or her own?

The car stopped but Richard made no attempt to get out. 'Good night, Kate,' he said.

She struggled with the door handle and, averting her eyes from the back seat, climbed out of the car.

'Night, Kate,' echoed Nella indistinctly, and there was a corresponding grunt from Martin.

They had driven away before her key found the lock.

'How did the view go?' Lana inquired the next morning. 'I see quite a few of the paintings are sold.'

'Everyone seemed pleased with it.'

Richard came in and dropped a small cellophane packet on Lana's desk. 'For Cinderella who couldn't come to the ball.'

'Oh, Mr Mowbray!' The deep flush again as Lana caught up the packet with trembling hands. It contained a rose, golden yellow, and a quick spray by the florist had resulted in a picturesque dewdrop nestling on its petals. Almost too perfect, Kate thought, and hated herself for her cynicism.

'Oh, thank you!' Lana was gushing. 'What a kind thought! It's beautiful!'

'I'm glad you like it. We thought of you last night, didn't we, Kate? We toasted absent friends.'

Kate felt he was involving her in some secret joke at Lana's expense. Yet it was kind of him to buy the flower. Why couldn't she accept that, instead of suspecting that he enjoyed fuelling Lana's devotion?

Michael phoned that evening. 'Kate, I'm tied up on Saturday. Could we make it Sunday this week?'

'Provided Josh is at the Minster by five o'clock.'

'Ah—that creates a problem. I was going to suggest you brought him up here. There's a model car exhibition which I'm sure he'd enjoy. Could he get special dispensation, do you think?'

Typical Michael, confident of bending the rules to his purpose. When she didn't speak, he said, 'Unless I hear from you, I'll assume it's OK. Eleven o'clock at the house?'

'Very well.'

Josh, who was eating his supper, broke into her thoughts. 'I had a note for you yesterday and I should have taken it back today. Mr Peters was cross.'

'I'm sorry, darling. What was it about?'

'A concert at school tomorrow. Auntie Madge is going and she said I can stay with Tim and Uncle Paul if you want to go.'

Madge herself phoned a few minutes later. 'I meant to mention the concert when I brought Josh back, but it slipped my mind. It's the older boys, of course, and some of them are quite brilliant. Paul's sorry to miss it but he has some homework to correct and it will save getting a babysitter. Since the next day's Saturday, I thought you mightn't mind Josh staying up a bit later than usual.'

So it was that Kate had her second evening out in the course of three days. The school was an impressive building fronting on Broad Street. It had been built in its present form towards the middle of the last century and its carved wooden panels and marble floors spoke of a more pretentious age. The hall where the concert took place was galleried, with a stage at one end. Madge and Kate took their places on the wooden chairs. There was a hum of conversation and rustling of programmes.

'If Josh shows any aptitude for an instrument,' Madge remarked, 'he couldn't be in a better place. They have outside teachers who come in to coach, famous names among them. As a result, the standard is extremely high.'

She was right. Kate hadn't known what to expect of the evening but she was unprepared for the effortless mastery the boys displayed over the intricacies of sonata and fugue, the sensitive violin-playing and the *élan* of the percussion. Having attended from a sense of duty, she was surprised at the extent of her enjoyment.

She and Madge walked home through a cool evening with a hint of mist. 'Autumn is well and truly here,' Madge said ruefully. 'Next stop, fireworks and Christmas!'

The light was on in the dining room and as they walked up the path they could see Paul seated at the table with exercise books spread around him. He came to the door to let them in.

'Are you stopping for coffee, Kate?'

'No, thanks, I'll go straight home. It's late enough for Josh, and I'm sure Madge wants to get Tim to bed.'

'I'll run you back, then.'

'No, please don't bother. We'll be home in less than ten minutes.'

Afterwards, she wondered how different events might have been if she'd accepted his offer.

Even in the few minutes it took to wean Josh from the television and button him into his mac, the mist had noticeably thickened. Auras hung round the street lamps, the garden gate was wet to the touch, and sounds were distorted. With Josh's hand firmly in hers, Kate walked quickly down Mead Way and along Gloucester Street. On the corner was a small public house—the Swan, judging by the creaking sign outside, and beneath it, huddled in their anoraks, stood a group of youths. The air was thick with the smell of fish and chips. The group made no attempt to let them pass, and perforce Kate stepped into the road, shepherding Josh in front of her.

She heard one of the boys give a snort of laughter and another said loudly, 'Good evening.' Kate did not reply, tried not to quicken her footsteps. As it was, Josh was almost running.

'I said, good evening, lady.'

'Good evening.' Stupid to feel nervous of them. They might even be boys from the school. But she knew they were not. The fitful street lamp had shone on the strangely obscene polished skulls of a bunch of skinheads.

Into Queen's Road now, with the crescent of Monks' Walk ahead and the Green to the right of them. To her horror, she heard footsteps fall in behind them.

'Walk you home, miss?'

'No, thank you. I haven't far to go.' Immediately she could have bitten her tongue. She had no wish for these youths to see where she lived, notice, perhaps, that the house was in darkness, so no large, reassuring husband awaited her return.

'Would the little boy like some fish and chips?'

'No, thank you.' Kate's heart was beating furiously and she was aware of the pale disc of Josh's anxious face turned up to her.

'Mummy, what do those boys want?'

'Nothing, darling, they're just being friendly.'

'What do those boys want, Mummy?' came a cruelly mocking echo. A roar of laughter greeted this sally.

'Bet Mummy knows, don't you, Mummy? Trouble is, finding it!'

'Are you going to be nice to us, then?'

Oh God, please let someone come along the road—anyone. Across the Green the silver mist rolled waist-high. Suppose they tried to force their way inside? Suppose-? She couldn't put into words what else they might do. How many were there? She daren't turn her head. Four or five, certainly. Possibly more.

Josh said plaintively, 'Can we slow down? I've got a stitch.'

Useless, then, to walk him past the familiar entrance and on to more certain safety.

Yet there was nowhere else she might take sanctuary. Surreptitiously, she fumbled in her handbag for the key. Best not to slacken pace in advance, but turn the key and slip inside in one movement. She said softly and rapidly, 'When I open the door, Josh, run straight upstairs and put all the lights on.'

'Hey—Mummy!' The raucous voice from behind. 'You haven't answered our question! Are you going to be nice to us?'

Fear made her desperate. She shot the key in the lock, pushed Josh inside and, jamming on the light, turned to face them. 'Leave me alone or I'll call the police!' she said.

Then she was inside, fumbling again with key and bolt which, mercifully, Martin had oiled for her. And all the while the hairless heads and grimacing faces were outlined at the glass, watching, gesticulating, their language increasingly explicit. She walked up the stairs without looking back, conscious of their eyes following her as far as the bend. Josh awaited her at the top in a blaze of light, eyes wide and frightened, and as she gathered him to her the doorbell pealed through the flat.

'I wish Daddy was here,' he said tremulously.

'If they ring again, I'll phone Uncle Paul. He'd be round in two minutes. But there's nothing to be frightened of, darling. They're only being silly.' Aren't they? Aren't they?

The bell chimed again but still she hesitated, reluctant to phone and admit her fright to Josh as well as to Paul. Loud voices called up to the window and as she drew the curtains there was an ironic cheer.

'They'll soon get tired,' she told Josh brightly. 'Come on, I'll make you a mug of hot chocolate and we'll go to bed.'

Blessedly, it seemed she was right. There was no more noise from below. They had only been amusing themselves, tormentors rather than vandals or worse. But if she'd lived farther away, if they'd had more time, what then?

Kate took a long time to go to sleep that night.

When Martin arrived the next morning, he picked up a duster without speaking and went straight out again.

'What was that for?' Kate asked when he returned.

'A four-letter word chalked on your door. Don't worry, it's gone now. Amazing what gives some people a thrill.'

Kate held down a spurt of fear. The boys would have forgotten the incident by now, and in the misty darkness they couldn't have remembered which doorway had been her bolt hole.

It was a pity Michael wasn't coming that day, to take Josh's mind off the previous evening. He was rather subdued and kept close to Kate's side.

'No fond papa?' asked Richard when Martin had taken the child to look at the paintings.

'No, I'm taking Josh to Shillingham tomorrow.'

'What will you do with yourself? Hardly worth coming back here, is it?'

'I haven't really thought.' But he had a point. It would be a waste of time to drive twenty miles back after leaving Josh, and then have to return to collect him.

'Tell you what, I'll meet you for a drink. I'll be home this weekend and it's only ten miles from Shillingham. We could have lunch if you like.'

Kate was conscious of Lana's averted head.

'It's kind of you, but I'm not sure what I'm doing yet.'

'Well, the invitation stands.'

Saturday proved busy as usual, with the paintings drawing extra crowds. Another couple were sold, three more reserved for consideration. At lunchtime Lana departed, not quite meeting

Kate's eyes as she wished her a happy weekend. It seemed Richard had deliberately made his suggestion in front of her, and Kate wondered to what end. Then she shook herself with a mental smile. She really must stop complicated motives to Richard. He was probably innocent of them all.

But though she hadn't accepted his invitation, he seemed to consider it confirmed. 'What time are you dropping Josh?' he asked towards the end of the afternoon.

'Eleven.'

'Then meet me at the King's Head at quarter past. The bar won't be open but they serve coffee in the lounge.'

'Richard, I—'

'Look, relax. I haven't any dastardly designs on you. It's simply that if you're at a loose end, it would help to pass the time.'

She flushed, feeling stupid. 'Yes, of course. Then, thank you.'

Thinking about the exchange later, Kate had the uneasy feeling that he had manipulated her as easily as he did Lana.

CHAPTER 10

Josh seemed relieved the next morning to be leaving Broadminster, and Kate couldn't blame him. The incident with the youths had not been mentioned again and she hoped it wouldn't linger in his mind.

'It'll be fun being home,' he prattled. 'I wonder if my plum stone's sprouting yet.'

'You'll soon see, won't you?'

'Are you coming to the museum with us?'

'No, dear. You and Daddy will enjoy it more than I would, and I've some things to do.'

He didn't press the point and when they turned into the familiar road and drew up at the gate, Kate found her eyes pricking. How many times had she walked up that path, in hope, excitement, happiness, and sadness. It seemed a parade of former selves passed before her eyes as she sat with her hands on the steering wheel. Josh meanwhile had scrambled from the car.

"Bye, Mum. See you later.'

At least she was 'Mum' again, after the frightened 'Mummy' of Friday evening. Michael opened the front door, and Kate thought she saw a shadowy figure behind him but could not be sure. Her mother-in-law, perhaps. She turned the car and drove slowly away. The church bells were ringing as the last late worshippers hurried up the path. The mist had gone this first Sunday in October and mellow sunlight lay richly on bronze and yellow leaf. All at once Kate was very grateful for Richard's offer of company. She would have been lost in this familiar place on such a strange occasion.

He was waiting for her in the coffee lounge and stood as she approached.

'You didn't change your mind, then. Good. Would you like a coffee?'

'Please.'

She sat on the plush-covered settee, her hands moving restlessly over its smoothness. Richard watched her for a moment.

'What time are you picking Josh up?'

'About five-thirty.'

'Then I suggest that instead of hanging around Sunday Shillingham, we drive out to Chipping Claydon. I'm a dab hand as a cook and can give you as good a meal as we'd get here.'

Twenty minutes later, as Richard manoeuvred his way out of town, Kate reflected how much of her past was bound up in Shillingham. She had come as a young bride, borne her son in the local hospital. This was the cinema to which they'd gone once a week until Josh was born, this the restaurant, albeit under new management, where in the early days they'd held hands under the table. She clenched her own hands and felt Richard glance at her.

'Memories, memories!' she said with forced lightness.

'The bane of our lives. I know.'

'I'm sorry. I was forgetting you've been through all this.'

He shrugged. 'It's behind me now. Never look back, they say, and it's good advice if you can take it. So let's try some forward thinking. I hope you'll like my home. I'm particularly fond of it, as heaven knows I must be, to stay there when I work thirty miles away!'

'Did you——?' Kate began, and stopped.

'Buy it when we married? No, fortunately, or I might have been persuaded to include my wife's name on the deeds. As it is, it's solely mine. I was driving through the village soon after leaving university, and I just looked up and saw it.'

'Looked up?'

'You'll see what I mean in a few minutes. I went straight to the nearest estate agent and told him that whenever that house came on the market, I wanted to buy it.'

'Without even looking over it?'

'I didn't need to.'

'And how long did you have to wait for it?'

'A couple of years, but I was quite content in lodgings, dreaming of when I could move in.'

'And when your marriage ended you weren't tempted to move away?'

'Positively not. I'd known the house longer than Christine.'

The rolling countryside was at its best in the wash of autumn colour. Woods, a tapestry of different shades, huddled in the hollows, chequered fields draped themselves over shallow hills. Five miles beyond Shillingham the road crossed over the motorway and shortly afterwards a sign to the right indicated that Chipping Claydon lay five miles ahead.

A few farm buildings lined the road. Pretty Charollais cows

grazed in the fields, roofs were newly thatched, five-barred gates freshly painted. There was a complacent air of well-being about the area, very different from the apologetic ambiance of Littlemarsh. They were already running into the village, and the glowing biscuit-coloured stonework proclaimed the nearness, in this northwest tip of Broadshire, to the Cotswold hills. They followed the road down a dip and into the village proper, postcard-pretty with its green and duck pond, its cluster of honey-coloured houses.

'Now,' said Richard with quiet satisfaction, 'look up.'

Obediently Kate raised her eyes and gave an involuntary exclamation. Just beyond the sweep of the village a bluff of land rose sharply on the left, fronted by a wall of sheer rock as though in some glacial age a piece had been sliced off it. And at the top of this bluff, some two hundred feet above the village, Kate could see the roof of a house.

'You live up there?'

'I do. It's known as The Look-out, for obvious reasons.' He branched to the left, following a narrow lane up the hill. There were a couple of cottages at the bottom, another halfway up. The lane, a *cul-de-sac*, ended at a white gateway.

'I'll open it for you.' Kate slipped out of the car. The breeze was fresh up here and lifted her hair. She closed the gate after Richard and he drove the few remaining yards to the circular sweep of gravel in front of the house. Kate looked about her. The garden had been left largely to its own devices—again a contrast to that in Littlemarsh—but a maritime flavour was evident in the bordering of seashells round the path, the coarse grass growing up the bank, and more particularly in the flagpole she could see behind the house.

Richard had got out of the car. 'Come and see the view.'

They walked round the side of the house. The garden at the back was not large and, in its open position, exposed to every wind. It was completely encircled by a stone wall at shoulder height, in front of which a telescope had been mounted. Kate leant on the warm stone, silent for a moment. Below her, the village of Chipping Claydon went about its Sunday business. Over the next rise she could see the farms they had passed, dwarfed to children's toys by height and distance, and beyond them the ribbon of the Shillingham road.

'It's—fabulous!' She turned smilingly and was disconcerted to find Richard closer than she'd expected. For a moment she met the clear, strangely expressionless eyes. Then he smiled and said, 'Let's go inside.'

She followed him to the front of the house and he unlocked the door. There was a minute hallway with steep narrow stairs and then they were in the long, low sitting room. The light inside was yellow, like artificial sunlight, and Kate saw that it came from bottle glass in the windows. Those on either side of the fireplace were small and round like portholes.

'As you might guess, it was built by a retired naval captain.'

'It's most unusual.' Kate looked about her and was immediately struck by a large, full-length portrait on one wall. She walked over and studied it. It was of a young woman, attractive but not beautiful, auburn-haired, and with a quizzical tilt to her head. It was so lifelike that, as with Sylvia's portraits, Kate felt embarrassed to be staring at it.

'My ex-wife,' said Richard behind her.

'It doesn't upset you, having it here?'

'Art is art, my dear. That happens to be a Bardin and worth a mint of money. There's no point in selling it out of sentiment, but when the time's right no doubt it will go under the hammer.'

'With no regrets?'

'With no regrets. They're a waste of time and energy.'

Yet according to Martin, Richard had been devastated by his wife's departure. At what cost had he achieved this apparent lack of emotion?

'Let me get you a drink. What'll it be?'

As he poured it, Kate continued her inspection of the room. There were some fine antiques—Chippendale tables, button-back chairs, small pieces of silver and ivory. On the wall by the fireplace hung an impressive display of edged weapons, and Kate remembered Martin telling her about them.

'Who does the dusting?' she asked with a smile.

'I have what is known as a treasure, Mrs Davies by name, who lives at the foot of the lane. She came when I first moved in and, since housework never appealed to my wife, continued during the five years of my marriage and beyond. Two mornings a week, year in, year out, and never a breakage yet.'

'A treasure indeed.' Kate took the glass he offered and his fingers brushed briefly against hers.

'Relax, Kate. You're still on edge.'

'I'm sorry.' She was impelled to add, in defence, 'It was coming back to Shillingham.'

'Love is the very devil,' Richard said lightly. 'Arranged marriages are much more sensible. Friendship, respect, affection; fine. One can remain in control. But once you allow yourself to love, even a goldfish, and you become a hostage to fate.'

The lunch he served was delicious and Kate told him so. He accepted her compliments impassively. 'I enjoy cooking,

101

it's therapeutic. I'm a great believer in therapy.' Again his eyes held hers, bland and uninformative, and as usual she hadn't the slightest idea what he was thinking.

'Josh will be envious when I tell him about this.' She was aware of speaking too quickly. 'Chicken is his favourite meal.'

'Josh,' Richard repeated consideringly. 'How did you come up with that name?'

'It was—just a private joke, and it stuck.'

'Concerning the walls of Jericho?'

She looked at him quickly and away again. 'Something like that.'

Oh God, what was she doing here with this enigmatic man? She felt he knew more about her than she might wish, but that was just being fanciful.

Over coffee the conversation moved from the personal to Pennyfarthings and the exhibition.

'I saw you talking to Sylvia Dane,' Richard remarked, lighting a cigar and leaning back in his chair. 'Is she a friend of yours?'

'I met her at Madge Netherby's.'

'Ah yes, the St Benedict sorority. Both their husbands teach there, I believe. She's an excellent artist, anyway.'

'Anyway?'

Richard laughed. 'Meaning that's all that concerns me.'

'Which in turn means—?'

'If she's a friend of yours I must watch my step, but I've heard she's rather free with her favours.'

'Really?' Not for anything would Kate have admitted prior knowledge.

'Tea and sympathy for gentlemen whose wives don't understand them.'

'I'm surprised you listen to gossip, Richard.'

'The spice of life, my dear, even if traditionally a feminine pursuit.' He paused. 'You know the origin of the word, of course?'

'Close woman friend,' Kate recited. 'Hence the gossip chair, with its wide seat to accommodate skirts.' She looked at him challengingly. 'Ten out of ten?'

'My dear Kate, you never disappoint me.'

'It's early days yet.'

The afternoon passed more comfortably with the help of the Sunday papers. But even those weren't wholly innocuous, commenting as they did on the continuing stalemate in the murder investigation. At five o'clock Richard drove Kate back to the King's Head where she'd left her car, and she dutifully thanked him for a pleasant day.

Her private estimation of it was more cautious. An interesting day, certainly, but in parts an uncomfortable one. She did not know what to make of Richard Mowbray, and the admission was beginning to needle her.

She turned into Lethbridge Drive as the church clock struck the half hour. As she drew up at the gate, the front door opened and Josh came running down the path followed by Michael.

'We've had a super time, Mum! The model cars were fantastic!'

Seeing Michael follow him out of the gate, Kate wound down her window and waited. He bent, dark eyes a little wary. 'All well, Kate?'

'Fine, thank you.'

'You managed to fill in this time? I should have—'

'Yes, indeed. I've been over at Richard Mowbray's. He has a fascinating house at Chipping Claydon.'

Michael's eyes flickered and he straightened. 'That's all right, then. No doubt I'll see you next Saturday.'

'No doubt.'

'Good-bye, Josh. Don't forget to give Mummy her letters, and take care of her.'

Kate started the car and drove slowly away, hoping she was not going to burst into tears. Beside her, Josh chatted incessantly of his day. It wasn't until they were some way down the Broadminster road that his words penetrated and her hands tightened on the wheel.

'Who did you say was with you?'

'Auntie Jill, Mum, I've been telling you. She let me help her make a cake.'

'At home?' Kate's voice cracked. 'She baked a cake at our house?'

'Yes, of course.' He paused and added by way of explanation, 'She's a friend of Daddy's. I told you.'

'So you did.' At least, Kate thought bleakly, Michael now knew that she too had been behaving like a free agent.

'Damn!' she said under her breath, and as her foot went down on the accelerator, the car sped towards Broadminster.

CHAPTER 11

The next morning incorporated all the worst aspects of a Monday. It was an effort to get out of bed. Josh couldn't find his maths book, the breakfast eggs cracked in the pan. It was ten to nine by the time they hurried out of the door, and Josh's insistence on stopping to feel in the letter box was an added irritation.

'See!' he exclaimed triumphantly, running after her down the road. 'There was something after all!' And he handed her a small packet. Kate slipped it in her pocket.

'You run on, Josh. Auntie Madge is waiting and I must get back.' She paused only long enough to see him join the others and, having already forgotten the packet, hurried back to the shop. It was only at lunchtime, back in the flat, that, feeling for a handkerchief, her fingers encountered something hard and she drew out the cardboard box.

Kate regarded it with surprise. Had that been in the letter box? It bore neither name, address, nor postmark. She lifted the lid and stared blankly at the contents. Filling the space inside was a large death's-head moth, the yellow skull clearly defined on the brown thorax. Wings, legs, and feelers had been detached from the body and each grisly piece anchored in place with sticky-tape. With a conscious effort of will, Kate replaced the lid and dropped the box in the bin.

Let it have been dead before it was dismembered, she thought fervently. But who could have left it, and why? Was it intended for Josh, a joke by some of his schoolmates? Yet this was no schoolboy prank. The gloating arrangement of the pathetic hair-like legs showed a cruelty that made her shudder. Though she hadn't touched the contents of the box, Kate washed her hands at the sink. She felt slightly sick, unable to imagine who—

She paused suddenly, towel in hand. The boys who'd pestered her on Friday? Surely their spite would have evaporated long since. She shrugged, resolving to forget the matter, but the outline of the skull remained in her mind for the rest of the day.

The art exhibition was continuing, and from time to time the artists called in to check their sales. Nella also came one morning, this time braving Lana's disapproval to stay for coffee.

'Who's sold the most so far?' she asked Kate, who was snatching a cup before going back outside.

'Daniel Plumb. All his were earmarked by the end of last week. And Sylvia's are going well too.'

'At least she has a ready supply of subjects,' Nella remarked. 'She should do a series, with the group title "These I have loved."'

Kate laughed protestingly. 'Oh come, now, she's not that bad.'

'How do you know? I shouldn't be surprised if she ran extra-mural classes for the senior boys! Poor old Henry, the husband's always the last to know.'

'Whose name are you blackening now, my love?' Martin came into the office and dropped a kiss on her golden head.

'Kate, that couple by the window are tempted by the Hawkins. See if you can swing the balance, will you?'

Richard had not put in an appearance that week, and despite herself Kate's mind kept returning to the hours they'd spent together on Sunday. Which, she told herself sharply as she prepared supper, was a singularly fruitless exercise.

Josh had been watching children's television and the signature tune of the early evening news broke into Kate's thoughts and, with the opening announcement, riveted them.

'There has been a fresh development in the so-called "Delilah killings" with the discovery this afternoon of the body of thirty-year-old Jane Forbes at her home in Larksworth. Mrs Forbes, whose divorce was widely reported two weeks ago, was stabbed to death in her kitchen, apparently while making bread. The word "Delilah" was again written in lipstick on the mirror. Broadshire police are appealing for information about any strangers seen in the vicinity, but their inquiries are hampered by the fact that Wednesday is market day in Larksworth and this draws people to the village from a wide area. Over now to Jack Stacey in Larksworth.'

Kate stood at the counter staring across at the policemen and dogs, the shocked neighbours in their doorways, till the fiercely hissing fat in the pan behind her recalled her to her surroundings and she returned to continue with the meal.

In her own kitchen, making bread. Planning, perhaps, to make some phone calls while it was rising, what to have for supper. Then suddenly, in that familiar setting, death. Kate shuddered. All three women had been killed in their homes, surrounded by friends and neighbours, and no one had noticed anything. It was more than surprising, it was terrifying.

She drained the spaghetti, poured the meat sauce over it, and called to her son. As she put the plate in front of him, the telephone shrilled.

'Madge here, Kate. I wondered if you'd like to come to Heatherton tomorrow? There's a new branch of Faversham's opening, with lots of special offers. Paul will bring the boys home, and you could stay for supper.'

'That sounds lovely.' This time, she'd let Paul drive them home.

'Come round when you close and we'll have lunch before we go.'

It was eleven-thirty at night and Webb had just returned from six gruelling hours in Larksworth, but Headquarters had a time scale all its own. The Incident Room was crowded with men chalking names on the blackboard, checking indexes, answering the almost continuous phone calls. In the midst of it all, Phil Fleming prowled restlessly, picking up statements, looking over shoulders. He turned as Webb entered.

'Come and sit down, Dave. Someone'll get you some tea. Any developments?'

Webb shook his head, lowering himself into the seat the Chief Superintendent pulled out. 'Not a thing out of anyone. She was chatting on the phone at two-fifteen. At two forty-five she was dead. And no one saw a goddamned thing.'

Fleming stretched out his legs, waiting while Webb sipped at the steaming tea. A pleasant-faced man with greying hair, he had the calm, soothing manner of a family doctor but his staff had long discounted it. The Chief Superintendent had a brain like a rapier and he expected his subordinates to be equally sharp-witted.

'There are the usual points of similarity,' he said as Webb put down his cup. 'Any notable differences?'

'Not that I can see.'

Fleming sucked in his cheeks. 'Let's talk the thing through, Dave. See if anything new hits us. Start with the Meadowes case.'

Webb wiped his hand over his face, widening his eyes to relieve the strain. 'Well,' he began, 'it looked at first as if she was killed by someone close to her, but that only held till the second murder. M.O. identical, so presumably the same killer, but surely a different motive. It was stretching it to suppose he was involved enough with *two* women to the point of murdering them. Yet they'd let him into their homes and the attacks obviously came out of the blue. No defence marks on any of them, including this last one. Now, God help us, we've got three bodies, and the only common denominator is that they were divorced women. As far as we know, they'd never met each other, didn't belong to the same club, frequent the same pubs, go on the same holidays. Hell, there's *nothing* that links them except the way they died.'

Fleming was listening intently, head slightly on one side like an intelligent bird. 'There's one other experience they shared: they'd all been mentioned recently in the press. Meadowes for her court appearance, the other two in connection with their divorces. Suppose, just suppose, the murderer uses the local rag to keep abreast of divorce cases and chooses his victims from that?'

Webb stared at him. 'You mean he might not even know them? Then why should they let him into their homes?'

'That's what we've got to find out.'

'Well, if that's his little game, we can soon put a stop to it. I'll get Romilly to withhold the names in all divorce cases till we give him the all-clear.'

'Let's hope Chummie hasn't an advance fixture list!' Fleming permitted himself a smile. 'And there's another point. The three deaths were not only similar, but identical, even to the position of the bodies. They were all *sitting down*. What does that suggest?'

Webb thought for a moment. 'That it wasn't just any old caller who'd come to the door and forced his way inside. It was someone they were prepared to spend some time with. Jane Forbes had even broken off her baking to make tea.'

'Precisely,' Fleming confirmed with quiet satisfaction. 'The caller was expected to stay for a while. It was worth sitting down, even making a cup of tea. So who could fit into that category?'

'The vicar?' Webb suggested with a lopsided grin.

'You're on the right track. Suppose it was not the man himself but his occupation which the women accepted? Meter reader, delivery boy, door-to-door salesman?'

'I doubt if any of that lot are invited to sit down, unless they're flogging encyclopaedias. We did check along those lines, people so familiar as to be almost invisible—postmen, paper boys, milkmen, and so on. Trouble is, not many of them are still around by the afternoon, and the Gas and Electricity Boards hadn't any men out at the time. Also, don't forget, Mrs Burke was killed on a Sunday. That narrows the field.'

'Back to the vicar, perhaps! It's incredible he wasn't seen entering or leaving any of the houses. In each case there were plenty of people about. Even on Sunday afternoon the neighbours would be working in their gardens or washing their cars.'

'And no one saw a thing.'

Fleming pulled reflectively at his lower lip. 'He must have his own transport. He might have managed without in Shillingham and Broadminster, but in a village everyone knows each other.

He wouldn't risk public transport even on market day unless he was a very cool customer. I know you've been through them dozens of times, Dave, but have the statements checked again to see if any one car, van, bike, anything crops up more than once.'

Webb made a note on the pad in front of him. 'There's another thing. Although all three women seemed to accept the visitor, he hadn't been expected. I can't vouch for Linda Meadowes, but Mrs Burke and Mrs Forbes were very methodical. There were engagement diaries hanging in both kitchens, and even a regular visit to the hairdresser was noted down. If someone had been expected, his name would have been there.'

'Unless we're back to the grocery order which was delivered every week.'

'Again, not on Sundays. And Mrs Forbes was the only one in her kitchen. The other two were in their front rooms, rather formal entertaining for the grocer's boy. Nor could it have been a doctor. They were all healthy and in any case didn't belong to the same practice.'

Fleming sighed. 'You know what's worried me all along? The fact that none of the victims was raped. Damn it, the word "Delilah!" places them fair and square in the category of sex murders and in all such cases there's assault of some kind, rape, mutilation, and so on. But our Delilah man contents himself with one neat, lethal incision and goes on his way.'

'Perhaps he just doesn't like women. Could be a homosexual.'

'That's a possibility. Widen your inquiries to take in any known gay communities. We might get a lead there. Is the press conference fixed, by the way?'

'Yes, nine-thirty in the morning.'

'Then I suggest we both get some sleep while we can.'

Amen to that, Webb thought wearily as he followed his superior out of the room.

'BROADSHIRE KILLER STALKS DIVORCED WIVES' proclaimed the papers the next morning. Kate averted her eyes and Lana smiled sympathetically.

'There's no getting away from it, is there?'

'That's how I feel. Last night I'd have given anything to get out, go to the cinema, anything to take my mind off it, but of course I couldn't.'

'I could sit for you on Thursdays,' Lana offered, 'while Mr Parsons is with Father.'

Kate smiled. 'That's sweet of you, but you mustn't give up your free evenings for me.'

'But I'd enjoy it—really. I'm fond of Josh and it would be a change for me too to get out of the house. If I could be sure of catching the last bus, I'd be pleased to come.'

Kate told Madge of the offer as they were driving to Heatherton.

'That's nice of her. Josh could always sleep at our place, but for a visit to the flicks it's hardly worth the upheaval.' She pulled in behind a lorry. 'As it happens, you're about to be honoured with an invitation to the Danes'. Sylvia mentioned it yesterday. I'll try to steer her towards a Thursday.'

On the right of the road Kate recognized the sprawling shape of The Duck Press restaurant. 'That's where we went after the private view.'

'Looks plush. How are you getting on with them all?'

'Martin's pleasant and easy-going, and Richard's not there very often.' She hesitated. 'Actually, I spent Sunday with him, while Josh was with Michael.'

'With Richard Mowbray?' Madge turned in surprise and the car swerved slightly. 'Well, well, you dark horse!'

'It seemed preferable to hanging round on my own or trailing back to Broadminster.'

'He's quite attractive, isn't he, in a pale, intense way.'

'I suppose so. Lana would agree. I told you she has a soft spot for him.'

'And have you?' Madge's eyes were on the road.

There was a pause, then Kate said consideringly, 'Not a soft spot, no, but I'm very aware of him.'

'Physically, you mean?'

'Yes.' Kate gave a strained little laugh. 'At least, I think so. Since I was eighteen there's never been anyone but Michael; I'm not used to standing back and considering men in that light.'

'More importantly, in what light is he considering you?'

'Probably none at all, but any intentions he might have will be strictly dishonourable. He's been through the divorce courts and he's no intention of letting anyone come too close.'

'He told you that?'

'More or less.'

They were running into the outskirts of Heatherton and fell silent as Madge threaded her way through the traffic to the car park.

It was a pleasant little town, not as large as Shillingham nor as old as Broadminster, but content with its own position in the county. It had a new shopping precinct, an ice rink, and a repertory theatre of which it was very proud. Kate and Madge window-shopped their way along, enjoying the change of scenes and making several small purchases. The new store when they reached it was attractively set out and they spent some time there, relaxed and laughing as they examined the more extreme fashions on display.

'There's no hurry to get home,' Madge remarked. 'Let's have a cup of tea.'

The café was crowded. They were met with a babble of conversation and the unmistakable smell of tea urns and buttered toast. There were no free tables but Kate spotted a couple of empty chairs and they made their way over. Seated at the table were two elderly women, grey hair tightly curled, faces flushed. They broke off their conversation as Kate and Madge sat down, but immediately one of them, catching Madge's eye, blurted out, 'There's been another murder. Have you heard?'

'At Larksworth? Yes, I know. I—'

'No, I mean *today*. There's been another today! A divorced woman again, in Otterford this time. It was on the billboards as we came in. Stop press, it said. Where's it going to end, that's what I'd like to know.'

Having deposited their bombshell, the women gathered together an assortment of string bags and shopping baskets and, nodding to the two friends, made their departure.

'Do you believe it?' Madge asked after a moment.

'I don't want to.'

'Surely they're mistaken? The billboard was probably left from yesterday.'

'Not if it said Otterford.'

The waitress appeared and Madge ordered a pot of tea. Neither of them had any appetite.

'It's not possible,' Kate said. 'Not two days running.'

'Perhaps he's working his way through the villages now. Better tell Lana to watch her step.'

'At least she's not divorced.'

On the car radio the news headlines confirmed the story. The body of Rose Percival, at twenty-five the youngest victim to date, had been found at home, et cetera, et cetera. No break-in, no robbery, the lipstick accusation. Delilah.

Paul met them at the door, his face drawn. 'Come into the dining room; I don't want the children to hear this.'

'Paul, what is it?' Madge clutched his arm in sudden fright.

'Nothing too terrible.' He closed the dining room door and stood leaning against it. 'Simply that I was there this afternoon. In Otterford.'

Madge moistened her lips. 'Why?'

'One of the boys wasn't well and Matron was under pressure. We're heading for a whooping-cough epidemic, by the way. So since I had a free period, I ran him home. God, Madge, that girl could have been someone I passed in the street. So could the murderer, come to that.'

'Is it a large village?' Kate asked.

'Fairly, and it was market day. Like yesterday in Larksworth.'

'That's why he struck again,' Madge said flatly. 'Crowds, and no one expecting another murder so soon.'

Paul glanced at the clock. 'Let's go and watch the news on the portable.'

It was cool in the bedroom. Kate was shivering as she sat on the bed, partly with the change in temperature, partly from apprehension. The opening headlines were a macabre echo from the previous evening, then Detective Chief Superintendent Fleming, solemn-faced, appeared on the screen.

'I see that a press report compares this killer with the Yorkshire

Ripper,' the interviewer was saying, 'obsessed not with prostitutes but unfaithful wives. Would you go along with this?'

'On the face of it, yes, but that doesn't mean everyone else is safe. This killer is extremely dangerous, able to talk his way into people's homes and then stab them before they realize they're in danger. I would strongly advise everyone to be on their guard. Don't let anyone into your home if you're alone, even if you think you know them. I can't stress enough that the murder victims also felt perfectly safe.'

Paul switched off the set, glancing from his wife's pale face to Kate's. 'Let's go and have a drink,' he said.

But the sombre mood stayed with them and they sat in silence, listening to the murmur of the children's voices from the kitchen. After a while Paul stood up and went to the window, his hands deep in his pockets as he stared out at the darkening garden. 'I keep trying to remember everything I saw after I turned off the main road. There might be something useful.'

'And what did you see?'

'Not much, till I came to the village. I was concentrating on young Beddowes, who was an unhealthy shade of yellow. There were a few cars and delivery vans, a moped. No doubt a lot of the market people were in Larksworth yesterday. It could be one of them, but I don't remember any names. The police will be following that up, anyway. I did notice a Telecom van, but I don't know how near it was to where Mrs What's-her-name was killed.' He laughed briefly. 'Perhaps someone is describing my car to the police!'

'In which case,' Kate advised, 'I should get your story in first.'

'*My* story?'

Madge said lightly, 'Don't get edgy, darling. We don't really think you did it.' 'Thanks.'

Even Madge's cooking couldn't raise their spirits. They ate almost in silence, hung over with disquiet. Kate remembered the words of the woman in the café: 'Where's it all going to end—that's what I'd like to know.'

Towards the end of the meal the three children, bored with being on their own, wandered into the dining room. Donna was holding a small box and Kate's reflexes snapped into action, surprising herself as much as the others.

'What's that?' she asked sharply, snatching it from the child's hand. Inside, under a lump of cotton wool, lay a tiny doll.

Donna gazed up at her wide-eyed. 'It's Debby's bed.'

'Yes, so I see.' Kate tried to steady her voice, aware of Paul and Madge's surprise.

'Where did the box come from, Donna?'

Madge said quietly, 'It had a brooch in it. Is anything wrong, Kate?'

Impossible to go into it all now. Kate shook her head and gave Donna a strained smile as she returned the box. 'It makes a cosy bed, doesn't it?' she said.

For seconds longer the tension held. Then Tim gave Josh a nudge and shouted, 'Bet I can beat you to the top of the stairs!' They thundered out of the room, closely followed by Donna, and the adults, after an embarrassed exchange of smiles, relaxed again.

Later that evening Richard phoned. 'Kate, I can't get hold of Martin, they must be out. Would you tell him I'll be back at midday tomorrow?'

'Of course.'

'How's the exhibition going?'

'Quite well. About half the paintings have been sold.'

'Should add up to a tidy little commission. See you tomorrow, then.'

Without analysing the reason, Kate felt her spirits suddenly lift. Humming softly to herself, she went in search of her novel.

CHAPTER 12

When Kate caught sight of Martin, she almost forgot Richard's message. There was a damp, unhealthy look to his skin, his eyes were sunken, and the usual boyish charm had vanished. Without it to belie the grey hair, he seemed ten years older.

'Whatever's wrong?' she exclaimed involuntarily. 'Are you ill? Shall I get a doctor?'

He raised a hand and attempted to smile. 'No, no, I'm all right. Haven't you seen a hangover before? We were out drinking last night and I rather overdid it.'

'Richard was trying to contact you. He asked me to tell you he'll be back at lunchtime.'

'Right. Thanks.'

She hesitated, not convinced of the explanation for his malaise. 'Would you like some black coffee?'

'To put it bluntly, I'd bring it straight back. I'll be OK if I take things quietly.'

The doorbell rang and with a last anxious glance at him, Kate went through to the shop. Sylvia Dane was standing there. 'Ah, Kate. Just the person I wanted. I've been trying to fix a date for you and the Netherbys to come for dinner. Madge tells me Thursday is your best day. Are you by any chance free next week?'

'I think I could be. Thank you.'

'We'll expect you at seven-thirty unless I hear from you. Now, to business. How many of my portraits are left?'

'Only one, the young girl. It had a reserved disc on for two days, but the purchaser changed his mind.'

'Well, five out of six isn't a bad score. I'll collect it tomorrow—or rather, Henry will.'

In a lull between customers, Kate put her head round the office door. 'Lana, could I take advantage of your offer to babysit next Thursday?'

Lana looked up without pausing in her rapid typing. 'Yes, of course.'

'Thanks so much. Mrs Dane has invited me for dinner.'

'I didn't know she was a friend of yours,' Lana said primly, and Kate smiled to herself. Someone else of whom Lana didn't approve.

Martin had disappeared and when he returned to the shop at three o'clock Richard was with him. While Martin made a phone call, Richard strolled over to Kate, who was setting out some new stock.

'Good afternoon, Mrs Romilly.'

'Hello.' She pushed her fingers down in the box, feeling among the crumpled paper and extracting a tissue-wrapped package. 'Is Martin better? He seemed under the weather this morning.'

'He's all right. The hair of the dog put him back on his feet.' Richard watched for a minute or two as she continued to unwrap the china. 'Do you enjoy working here?' he asked suddenly.

'Of course.'

'It's not very high-powered for one of your abilities.'

She looked up, unsure whether he was goading her, but as usual his eyes were expressionless. 'It's exactly what I need at the moment and I'm very grateful to have it.'

'Till something better turns up.'

'That wasn't what I meant at all. I have the flat, I'm near Josh, and I'm perfectly happy.'

'Still, we don't want you to get bored playing shop, do we? I have to go to Yorkshire on business shortly. Why not come along?'

Kate sat back on her heels and looked up at him. The hazel eyes, curiously intent, waited expectantly.

'Josh could stay with your friend for a couple of nights, I'm sure.'

'What about the shop?'

'Martin can cope. Anyway, you don't have to make a snap decision. Think it over.' And he strolled away, leaving Kate looking thoughtfully after him.

Michael was late the next morning. Josh, tired of his drawing, wandered round the office picking things up and getting in the way. Lana didn't seem ruffled but Kate, busy with the last day of the exhibition, felt guilty at leaving him with her.

'Why don't you wait upstairs, dear?' she suggested at last. 'Daddy must have been delayed.'

'It's silly, not living with him anymore,' Josh said rebelliously. Kate felt herself go hot. This was the first time he had questioned the change of circumstance.

Aware of Lana's attention, she said carefully, 'I did explain, darling, about school and Daddy's job.'

'Other boys live in Shillingham and come on the train every day. Why can't I do that? I like trains.'

'We can think about it. Now—'

But Josh was not going to be distracted. 'When are we going home?' he persisted. 'I've hardly any toys here and I want to play with my trains.'

'We'll go and get them now, if you like.' Michael was standing in the doorway.

Josh's face lit up. 'Can we, Daddy?'

'I don't see why not. You should have mentioned them last weekend, though. I'd thought of the cinema for today.'

'Can we go to the cinema and *then* go for my trains?'

Michael shook his head. 'Sorry, old chap. There wouldn't be time.'

'I don't see—' Josh began, but Michael's eyes had gone to the two women. Kate tried to collect herself.

'I don't think you've met my husband, Lana. Michael, Lana Truscott.'

Michael took her hand with the charm which stood him in such good stead. 'I'm delighted to meet you. I hear you live enviably surrounded by all manner of animals!'

Lana laughed, and with a shock Kate realized it was the first time she'd heard her. 'The country has some compensations.'

Josh was tugging at Michael's jacket. 'Daddy, why do we have to stay here? When are we coming home?'

'You'd better ask Mummy,' Michael said evenly.

When they had gone, Kate said defensively, 'That's the first time Josh has even hinted at not being settled here.'

'Your husband's very charming, isn't he?'

'Oh yes,' Kate answered with unusual bitterness. 'He could charm the birds out of the trees.' And she went quickly back to the shop.

That evening, Michael was waiting with Josh when she went to answer their knock. Josh brushed past her and wandered up the stairs and Michael said drily, 'It's all right, I'm not coming in. I just wanted to tell you no more was said about going home. He was only playing you up.' He paused. 'I thought you might have been worrying about it.'

'Yes, I was. Thank you.'

Michael glanced at her and then away down the length of Monks' Walk. 'You've been here a month now. Any nearer reaching a decision?'

'No.'

'Fair enough.' He straightened and turned to the car. 'I don't think much of your boss, by the way.'

'Which one?'

'The one you went waltzing off with last Sunday. He stared right through me this morning.'

'He probably didn't recognize you.'

Michael snorted and, grinding his cigarette under his heel, got into the car. After a moment Kate closed the door.

Kate and Josh spent their Sunday morning exploring Broadminster, and as Lana opened the mail the next morning, Kate told her of their latest discoveries.

'We came back across the Green,' she finished. 'There was a group of Japanese setting up their cameras to photograph Monks' Walk. I felt quite proud to be living here!'

Lana looked up quickly. 'Did you happen to notice anyone on those seats?'

'On the Green? No, why?'

'Oh, it—doesn't matter.'

'Lana, what is it?'

'Just that there's a man who spends a lot of time there. I wondered if you'd seen him, that's all.'

'What kind of man?'

'Nothing out of the ordinary. I only noticed him because not many people sit alone. Not of his age, anyway.'

'Which is?'

She shrugged. 'Thirties, I suppose. Forget it, Kate. It just struck me that from where he sat, he'd have a good view of this building.'

'And the rest of Monks' Walk, presumably.'

'Yes. Yes, of course. I'm being silly.'

'Which seat is it?' Kate asked after a moment.

'Just the other side of the pathway. The wall curves round and it's angled so that it faces this way.'

Kate went through the shop and out into the street. At this time in the morning only one of the seats was occupied, that which Lana had described. The man sitting there was obscured behind the newspaper he was reading. All she could see above and below it was a shock of dark hair and a pair of faded jeans. She hesitated, wondering whether to go closer, but an elderly man had stopped beside her with a shy smile.

'Good morning. Are you open, or am I too early?' And she had no option but to go with him back into the shop.

'Black hair and faded jeans?' Kate asked briefly, when she was free to return to the office.

'I beg your pardon? Oh, yes. Yes, that's right. Is he there again?'

'He was when I looked. When did you first see him?'

'About a week ago. Kate, I'm sorry if I worried you. It was just what it said in the paper, that houses may be watched to see who lives there, their movements and so on.'

'Yes,' said Kate. When next she looked, the seat was empty and she felt relief. It was probably nothing anyway.

The shop seemed bare without the paintings and Kate spent some time that week rearranging displays in the additional space. Though she kept glancing at the seat on the Green, she did not see the man in jeans again. This reassured her, till she wondered if he now had all the information he needed.

On the evening of the dinner party, Lana was at the flat by seven-fifteen. Kate watched with amused affection as she drew off her gloves and slipped them in her pocket. Catching Lana's eye, she said with a smile, 'When I was little, I was told it was ladylike to wear gloves, but I never think of them unless there are six inches of snow outside.'

Lana said defensively, 'I read the paper on the bus and they keep the print off my hands.' A flush coloured her cheeks. 'But that's not why I wear them,' she added quietly. 'You'll think it silly, no doubt, but it's to hide the fact that I haven't a wedding ring.'

'Oh, Lana!' Kate said softly, ashamed of her previous amusement.

'I know, I know. In this day and age, career women, and so on. That's all very well if you're confident and attractive and it's obvious you're unmarried from choice. But that,' she ended with a tight little smile, 'hardly applies to me.'

At a loss for words, Kate touched her arm sympathetically and took her up to see Josh. 'Here's Miss Truscott now. You'll be a good boy, won't you, and not give her any trouble.'

'What a nice room,' Lana said easily. 'I wish I had a skylight. Look, you can see the stars through it.'

Josh glanced up without much interest. 'Sometimes the moon shines on my face and wakes me up.'

'I know a story about the moon. Would you like to hear it?'

He eyed her warily. 'There aren't any fairies in it, are there?'

Lana laughed. 'Not one, I promise.'

'All right, then.'

She sat down on the bed and Kate turned to the door. 'Your bus goes at ten-thirty, doesn't it? I'll be back in good time—and thanks again for coming.'

The Danes lived less than five minutes away and Kate had only to follow the curve of Monks' Walk to the section near the school. The house was of weathered brick with the square sash windows of the Georgian period, boldly outlined in white paint. A short path led to the front door, which was set in a recess. Kate could hear voices in the hall and the door opened as she touched the bell.

'Come in, come in!' Henry Dane said heartily. 'You've all arrived together—splendid!'

Madge and Paul were just removing their coats and Sylvia came bustling up, exclaiming perfunctorily over the small box of chocolates which Kate handed her. 'Take them in, Henry, and pour drinks while I put something in the oven. I shan't be a moment.'

The sitting room ran from the front to the back of the house. The walls were a soft duck-egg blue and the carpet, deep and shaggy, only a shade darker. At the far end, glass doors led to a loggia, where Kate could see an easel.

'Sylvia's studio,' Henry confirmed, noting her glance. 'The north light and all that, but it cost a bomb to have it double-glazed to use in winter.'

As they settled down, Kate surreptitiously studied her hosts. Henry looked to be in his mid-fifties, balding, bespectacled, with the air of benign absentmindedness often seen in academics. His wife couldn't have been more than ten years younger, but time and cosmetics had treated her kindly and as an artist she knew which colours most became her.

'Cigarette, Kate?'

Sylvia leant forward with a silver box and the lamplight fell on her soft hair. Kate shook her head. 'No, thank you.'

'Good girl,' said her hostess complacently, lighting one herself. 'I keep telling myself I'll give them up, but I never do.'

Henry, sitting beside Kate, asked about her work, carefully avoiding any reference to her marriage. Kate wondered what Madge had told them.

'Your son shows an admirable grasp of algebra,' Henry was saying. 'I'm recommending he moves into the top set next term.'

'No shop, Henry, for God's sake!' Sylvia said impatiently.

'But I'm interested,' Kate defended him. 'I was wondering how Josh was settling down.'

'Admirably, I'd say, but there's an open evening at half term when you'll be meeting the staff. I'm sure you'll find you have no problems.'

'That's a relief, I must say!' Kate turned smilingly to Paul, but he wasn't listening. He was staring across at Sylvia, and, following his gaze, Kate was in time to see her smile and give an almost imperceptible nod. Instinctively Kate looked at Madge, but she was bending to stroke a small cat that arched against her legs. Beside her, Henry was still bumbling on about maths. It seemed only she had witnessed that oddly significant exchange, and Kate was relieved when it was time to go through to dinner.

'Have you been to Heatherton lately?' Madge was asking as Sylvia passed her the vegetables. 'Faversham's have a new branch there. Kate and I went last week. In fact, it was there that we heard of the latest murder, and when we got home, we found Paul had actually been at the scene of the crime.'

'So I believe,' Sylvia said. 'It must have been quite a shock.'

Madge looked at her in surprise. 'You'd heard?'

'Er—yes, I—'

'Of course, Henry'd have told you. It must have been all round school.'

'Yes, indeed,' Sylvia confirmed smoothly, and it was Kate who, not quite knowing why, breathed a small sigh of relief.

Over coffee in the sitting room, the talk was of poetry, a great interest of Henry's. 'It appeals to the mathematical brain,' he announced with heavy humour. 'I suppose you two young ladies have never heard of Hubert Rance?'

'I have,' Kate declared. 'He's one of the few modern poets I enjoy.'

'Is that so? And did you know he was a St Benedict's boy? In my form at one stage. I have an autographed book upstairs. I'll look it out before you go. You might like to borrow it.'

'I'd love to,' Kate said sincerely, 'and as a matter of fact I really should be going now. I don't want to break up the party, but Lana Truscott is babysitting and she has to catch the last bus home.'

'So soon?' Sylvia protested.

'In that case, I'll see if I can lay my hands on that book,' Henry said. As he left the room, Sylvia also rose. 'If no one wants more coffee, I'll clear it away.' She lifted the tray. 'Will you open the kitchen door for me, Paul?'

They went out together and Madge and Kate exchanged a smile.

'Enjoy yourself?' Madge asked.

'Very much. It was kind of them to invite me.' She looked at the clock on the mantelpiece. 'I really must go, though. I'll tell Henry not to bother about the book.'

She went into the hall, intending to call to him. On her right the kitchen door stood open and instinctively Kate glanced inside. Paul and Sylvia were standing close together, talking in low voices. Her hand was on his arm and his head bent attentively toward her. Though Kate hadn't made a sound, they turned at the same moment and moved swiftly apart. Sylvia came quickly to the door.

'You really have to go, Kate? What a shame. It's been lovely to see you.'

Kate glanced at Paul. He was watching her anxiously and gave a rather forced smile. She said clearly, 'Thank you so much. I have enjoyed it. Will you tell Henry—'

But Henry was coming heavily down the stairs. 'Sorry,' he said, 'I can't seem to find it. I'll dig it out for you and drop it in sometime.'

More thanks, more good nights, and the door opened to the cool October night. Paul suggested walking back with her, but Kate declined the offer. At that moment even the skinheads were preferable to a five-minute walk with Paul. But she was fortunate. She saw no one on the brief journey and, as she let herself into the flat, pushed all conflicting thoughts aside and went up the stairs to relieve Lana.

CHAPTER 13

I had to take them out again. I try not to, because of their effect on me—sweating, twitching, shaking. And—other things.

There's a pile of cuttings now. By the time I'd read them, I could hardly breathe. Yet I'm calm enough when it matters. Like a surgeon cutting out a cancer.

Which is what they are, these women. No loyalty, no morals, only self-indulgence. Like Sandra, and Christine, and—no, don't think that.

Michael Romilly. Quite a coincidence, when he writes so much about me. Does he guess we've met?

I've decided who'll be the next one.

My hands aren't shaking anymore. I must put the cuttings away.

CHAPTER 14

Paul's unaccountable behaviour filled Kate's thoughts the next morning and she didn't care for the direction they were taking. She was still brooding about it when she went out at lunchtime, and only realized Martin was behind her when he caught her arm.

'Hey, wait for me! You are in a brown study this morning!'

She forced a smile. 'Sorry, did you want me?'

'Just wondered what you were doing for lunch?'

'I'll have a sandwich when I get back. I've a lot of shopping—'

'Nonsense, you can't keep going on a sandwich. Come and eat with me.'

Despite her shopping list, Kate was easily persuaded, glad of the chance to be distracted from her worries. Martin took her to the Coach and Horses, where they'd lunched her first day at Pennyfarthings. Now, in mid-October, a fire was burning, its red gleam reflected in the horse brasses that framed the brick hearth.

They were halfway through their meal and Kate was pleasantly relaxed when the door opened with a rush of cold air and four men came in. One of them, large and red-faced, glanced in their direction, hesitated, and came over.

'Cheers, Martin old lad. Had your fingerprints taken?'

'Hi, Bill.'

'Thought I might have seen you at the nick, "helping with inquiries." How did it go?'

Kate glanced inquiringly at Martin and was startled to see the colour drain from his face. He said jerkily, 'I don't know what you mean, but my food's getting cold, so if you don't mind—'

'You owned up, surely? It'd be pretty damn risky not to.'

Martin moistened his lips. 'Bill, I told you. I haven't the faintest idea—'

'I'm talking, my lad,' the other man cut in with heavy emphasis, 'about the Otterford murder. Everyone who was there was asked—'

'But I *wasn't* there, for God's sake! What is this?'

The man called Bill stared at him. 'Now look, friend, I *saw* you! You were right beside me at the traffic lights, as close as you are now.'

There was a taut, prickly silence. Martin sat unmoving, still gripping his fork, whilethe other man stared down at him. Then Bill gave a shrug. 'OK, suit yourself. You've got a bloody double then.' And he turned away to join his friends at the bar. Kate saw him say something and they all turned and looked across. Martin still hadn't moved.

'What was all that about?' she asked uneasily.

'Search me.' As if her voice had dispelled his paralysis, he reached for his glass and drained it.

'You weren't really there, were you?'

'Of course I wasn't. What would I be doing in a dump like Otterford?'

If a reason occurred to Kate, it was one she could hardly put forward.

Martin said abruptly, 'I need another drink. Will you have one?'

She shook her head as he lumbered to his feet and made for the end of the bar farthest from Bill and his friends. When he returned it was with neat whisky instead of his usual pint, and he tossed it back in one gulp, wiping his mouth with the back of his hand. He looked ghastly, Kate thought with concern. A muscle was jerking at his eye and his face had the unhealthy tinge she'd noticed—

Her thoughts broke off in disarray and her mouth went dry. That morning when he'd looked so ill and dismissed it as a hangover—hadn't that been the day after the Otterford murder?

They were avoiding each other's eyes and it was a relief when Martin pushed back his chair. 'I've got to go and see someone,' he mumbled as they reached the pavement. 'I might not be back by closing time.'

'All right.' Kate watched him hurry away up the street, trying to make sense of what had happened. Unless Bill had made a genuine mistake—and from Martin's reactions, she didn't think he had—Martin had indeed been in Otterford that afternoon and was patently anxious to conceal the fact. Why?

Somewhere a clock struck two and she started hastily back to Monks' Walk. No time now to do her shopping, which meant braving the Saturday crowds tomorrow. A pity she hadn't stuck to her plan, thereby saving herself not only the disquieting incident over lunch but the doubts and questions it left in its wake.

And that afternoon she'd plenty of time to consider them. Hardly anyone called at the shop and eventually, determined to occupy her mind more fruitfully, Kate took out a book on porcelain which she'd been reading the previous week. Her place was marked with a slip of paper, hastily torn from the phone pad when the shop bell had interrupted her, and it was this improvised bookmark which now catapulted her into a new dimension of fear. For at the top of the sheet was a scrawl in Martin's writing. 'Mrs Percival, 2.30,' it read, and, underneath: '3 Westfield Close, Otterford.' Rose Percival, the youngest 'Delilah' victim.

For long minutes Kate stood staring at it, till the writing blurred and ran together, obscuring the message. Bill's voice said in her head, 'You owned up, surely?' And Martin's: '*I wasn't there!*'

Oh God! she thought numbly. And again: Oh God! Though aware of urgency, she was incapable of speedy reactions. It was an effort to lift the phone book, to search through the flimsy pages for the number of the police station. She still hadn't found it when a sound made her look up to see Martin standing in the doorway.

Frantically she marshalled her defences. 'I've phoned the police. They'll be here any minute.'

He said heavily, 'I've just left them. You can check, but they'll confirm it.'

'And they—?'

'Let me go?' He smiled, a travesty of his usual charming grin. 'God, Kate, I'm sorry. I shouldn't have let you go through this.' And as she still sat frozen, he added baldly, 'You can relax. I didn't kill her.'

Her eyes hadn't left him. 'It wasn't only the man in the pub.

I found this.' She pushed the incriminating note across the desk towards him.

'Hell, yes. I'd forgotten I wrote it down. But it was Tuesday, Kate. Lana'll confirm that. She was here when I took the call. The name rang a bell and she remembered the divorce had been in the papers. The husband had a nervous breakdown or something. I did go to see her, but on the Tuesday. Two days before she was killed.'

'Yet that man—'

'Saw me on the Thursday.' He seemed to have taken on himself the ending of sentences she couldn't finish. 'That's true. I was there, but I didn't kill her.'

He came forward and slumped into a chair, fumbling for a cigarette. It took several attempts to light it. 'She rang here last Monday,' he said, then: 'Just a routine call. Had a bit of silver she wanted me to look at. So I jotted down her address and went along.' He swallowed. 'She—God, she was dynamite! Something just flared between us—I could hardly keep my hands off her. It was mutual—she didn't try to hide it. If it hadn't been that her bloke was in the kitchen writing some report—' He broke off, drawing avidly on his cigarette and swallowing the smoke. 'Anyway, as I was leaving she told me he'd be away on Thursday and suggested I went back then.'

Kate sat motionless, watching him. He leaned forward and tapped some ash into a tin lid on the desk. 'I'm not proud of myself, Kate. I was a bloody fool and I know it, but well, I couldn't stop thinking of her. She really got me going. So I thought, what the hell? And I did go back. I went back and no doubt Bill Findlay saw me, but that was all, I swear it. Because I suddenly got cold feet, qualms of conscience, call it what you like. The upshot was I didn't even get out of the car. Turned round and hightailed it back home. But I can't prove it.'

He bent forward suddenly, his head in his hands. 'I keep imagining it all. She'd hear the bell and think it was me, because she was expecting me.' His shoulders heaved and Kate watched him with uncomprehending pity. Then he sat up and ran a hand across his face.

'Of course I should have told the police, but since I couldn't prove anything, I thought they might keep me in for questioning. Then what would I tell Nella? All right, I should have thought of that before. Of course I should; I just lost my head. But God, Kate, if I *had* gone, if I'd kept the appointment, she mightn't have been killed. I can never forget that.' After a moment he added flatly, 'Lord knows if the cops believed me. They wrote it all down and I signed the statement. It's anyone's guess what happens now.'

Out in the shop the doorbell chimed and Josh's voice called, 'Mum? Are you there?'

He seemed to come from another world. Kate tried to rouse herself. 'Yes, darling. Come through.'

Martin heaved himself to his feet and passed Josh in the doorway. Kate remained sitting at her desk, listening to Josh's rush of chatter. She was remembering that Paul had also been in Otterford that Thursday afternoon.

'What do you make of Bailey's statement?'

Sergeant Jackson looked up. 'He could have done it. He had the opportunity. But according to him, his only reason for going back was to have it off with her, and there's no evidence of that.'

Webb grunted. 'We've only his word that they fancied each

other. If he *is* Chummie, there wouldn't have been any hanky-panky, there never is. He's in the house less than ten minutes—maybe less than five. In Mrs Forbes's case her boyfriend was talking to her on the phone at two-fifteen and she was found at two-forty. Yet she was sitting at the kitchen table with two cups of tea in front of her. God, Ken, these murders are really getting to me. It's as though the bugger's sitting back thumbing his nose at us, and we can't do a damn thing about it.' He snapped the folder shut on Martin Bailey's statement. 'Anyway, file this for now, but we'll continue to bear him in mind. Don't forget he'd never have come in if he hadn't met someone who saw him there. Despite his glib explanations, that's not the action of an honest man.'

The following morning Michael collected Josh as usual and at lunchtime Kate went out to do her shopping. As she'd expected, the streets were crowded with weekend shoppers who strolled leisurely along the pavements and constantly slowed her progress. It was as she skirted one such group that Josh's indignant shout recalled her attention and she turned to see him standing with a red-haired girl who looked faintly familiar.

'Didn't you see me, Mummy?' he demanded in an aggrieved tone.

'I'm sorry, darling, I was too busy thinking what to buy for supper.' Her eyes moved from her son's upturned face to that of the girl beside him. She had coloured but her eyes, large and brown, met Kate's steadily.

'Hello, Mrs Romilly,' she said. 'I'm Jill Halliday. I work with your husband.'

Kate drew in her breath, but before she could reply Michael

emerged from a doorway, slipping a packet of cigarettes into his pocket. He looked swiftly from Jill to Kate. 'I don't believe you've been introduced. Jill works—'

'Yes—I know.'

Unaware of his elders' embarrassment, Josh said eagerly, 'We're just going for some Chinese, Mum. Would you like to come?'

'I can't, Josh. I must do my shopping. See you later, darling,' and with a jerky little nod in the direction of the other two, Kate went quickly up the road. So that was 'Auntie Jill' who was so much at home in Kate's kitchen. Perhaps she'd actually moved in with Michael.

The disquiet caused by the chance meeting gnawed at Kate all afternoon. It was not that Jill was with her husband and son that upset her, so much as the girl herself. The brief glimpse in Shillingham had left Kate with the impression of a cheap little flirt. She saw now that it was mistaken. Today she had met an attractive, serious-faced young woman, and Michael's association with her took on a new and disturbing significance.

In fact, the week had proved a watershed for Kate. During the course of it the people who surrounded her had subtly altered, throwing her assessment of them out of focus. Martin, still pale and withdrawn, was no longer the easy-going man he'd seemed. Paul, whom she'd thought she knew so well, had behaved out of character, and now Jill Halliday loomed as a serious contender for Michael's affections, casting Michael himself in a different light. Kate felt she was looking at them through distorting mirrors, no longer sure of any of them.

'Does Auntie Jill always come down with Daddy?' she asked with studied casualness as she and Josh were having supper. He shook his head.

'Just sometimes?' Kate persisted.

'First time,' corrected Josh with his mouth full.

'You didn't mind sharing Daddy with her?'

He looked up at her innocently. 'She asked me that too. No, I didn't mind. I like her. She's nice.'

'Yes, she—seemed to be.'

Later that evening Kate received the first anonymous phone call. Her mind still on Michael, she illogically assumed it was he who was calling and hurried to answer it.

'Hello—yes?'

Total silence greeted her, but it was a living silence. Someone was on the end of the line.

'Hello?' Kate said again, and after a moment gave her number. There was no response, just a palpable lack of sound. Kate stood waiting and eventually there was a little click as someone, somewhere, replaced the receiver. Shakily she followed suit. A wrong number, she told herself, returning to the kitchen, but the thought carried no conviction. If it had been, the caller would have realized at once, and either apologized or rung off. That deliberate waiting, the refusal to answer, implied a specific intention of—what? Intimidation? Was this the next phase of harassment from, presumably, those strangely persistent skinheads? Or had someone dialled completely at random, from sheer mischievousness? That must be the explanation. Nothing else made sense.

That Sunday was the third in the month and Josh and his fellow choristers were required at morning service. In accordance with instructions, he left early for a brief rehearsal and Kate, with time in hand, started to clean the flat. Her thoughts were still circling round Michael, and it was only when a peal of bells rang out that she realized she'd barely time to get to the service.

Catching up her handbag, she went running out of the flat, and reached the path to the Minster just as Paul came quickly round the corner of Queen's Road. Kate slowed to a halt, but instead of crossing towards her, he turned into the far end of Monks' Walk, went briskly along it as far as the Danes' house and, with a quick glance over his shoulder, turned into the gateway.

Kate stood staring after him till the strident chimes of the single bell sent her running up the path and through the great doorway. Someone put a book in her hand and showed her into a pew. Immediately in front of her Madge, well into the first verse of the hymn, turned and smiled at her, and across the aisle Kate recognized the grey, balding head of Henry Dane.

'Tea and sympathy,' said Richard's voice, 'for gentlemen whose wives don't understand them.'

And Madge's: 'Sylvia's involved with someone at school.'

Through the looking-glass, Kate thought despairingly. Nothing and no one as they seemed.

She would have liked to avoid Madge when the service was over, but of course that was impossible. She was waiting as Kate emerged from the door.

'You cut it rather fine, didn't you? I was trying to keep a place for you but I had to give it up in the end.'

Kate said carefully, 'Doesn't Paul darken the doors these days?'

'He opted out today. He's behind with some marking and it seemed a good chance to get on with it, while the house was quiet.'

Donna was scuffing her shoe on the gravel path. In her hand she held the little box which had such unpleasant associations. A doll's bed, Kate reminded herself. What else had she expected?

'Did you see Michael yesterday?' Madge asked in a low voice.

'Briefly.'

'You seem a bit strained. Nothing went wrong, did it?'

'He brought his girlfriend with him.' Which should explain her edginess, Kate thought with bitter gratitude.

Madge laid her hand on her arm. 'I'm sorry, love.'

Kate bit her lip and looked away. Dear Madge, with her gentle face and compassionate eyes, so unshakably confident of the stability of her own marriage. Kate glanced towards the Danes' house but Monks' Walk was now crowded with boys as the boarders returned to school. For Madge's sake, and hers alone, Kate hoped that by now Paul was safely home, surrounded by corroborative papers.

Mindful of her unfulfilled promise, Kate took an early opportunity to invite Lana for supper.

'I'd love to, Kate. How kind! And don't forget I can come any Thursday to babysit. Didn't you mention a parents' meeting coming up soon?'

Kate hesitated. 'It's next week, but I didn't like to ask again so soon. I was going to leave Josh with the Netherbys.'

'There's no need for that. Of course I'll come.'

Kate's thanks were interrupted by Richard's arrival. 'Lana, my love, will you do something for me?'

'Of course, Mr Mowbray.' The usual deepening of colour.

'I've drafted a letter to Simpson and Maybrick about the blue Worcester. Knock it into shape, will you. Can you decipher my writing?' He leaned over, reading the letter through with her, and Kate could see the rapid rising and falling of Lana's breast under the ungainly sweater. He was doing it on purpose, she thought resentfully, and it wasn't fair.

Richard looked up suddenly, met her accusing gaze, and closed one eye in a wink. Kate turned on her heel and left the room. Minutes later he followed her.

'Do I detect a hint of disapproval?'

'I think it's unkind of you to goad Lana like that.'

'Really?' He raised one eyebrow. 'I was under the impression that she enjoyed it.'

Kate didn't reply. She was finding that she wasn't immune to his closeness herself and wondered if he knew that too. They might all laugh at her as well as Lana.

It seemed politic to warn Josh of Lana's coming, since she was sure to want to see him.

'Will I have to listen to a soppy story?' he demanded truculently.

'Perhaps, but be kind to her, Josh. I think she's fond of you. She'll be coming to—sit for us next Thursday, too.' She didn't dare use the compound verb in his hearing. He muttered something under his breath, but when Lana returned from seeing him, Kate could tell by her smile that all was well.

'He's sharp as a tack, that one!' she commented, smoothing her skirt as she sat down. She was wearing a plain black jumper with a cameo at the throat and a black wool skirt patterned with cabbage roses. 'He'll be a handful when he's a little older, I daresay.' Her eyes, large and vulnerable, met Kate's briefly as she accepted a glass of sherry. 'But by that time,' she added quietly, 'all being well, you'll have your husband to back you up.' When Kate didn't speak, Lana leant forward impulsively.

'You will go back to him, won't you? I know it's none of my business but I'm so fond of Josh and I've seen what broken marriages can do to a child.'

'Your brother's little girl? But that was more than a divorce, wasn't it? I don't think you can—'

Lana made a sweeping gesture with her hand. 'Not just Judy. My brother himself—and me.' She drew a difficult breath. 'Our own mother left us when we were small. That's why I feel so strongly about it.'

'But I haven't left Josh,' Kate pointed out, trying to keep her voice reasonable. A lecture on marital fidelity was not what she'd anticipated.

'You've split up the family, and the damage can be long-lasting, you know. I read that children of divorced parents are more likely to have broken marriages themselves.'

Kate said with determined lightness, 'Statisticians can prove anything they put their minds to.'

'It was true in Ralph's case. And in Mr Mowbray's.'

'Richard's?' Surprise rang in Kate's voice. 'I didn't know his parents were divorced.'

'How should you? We were talking about it once, at the time of Ralph's death. I can't tell you how kind he was, how sympathetic. The tragedy seemed to bring us much closer, somehow.' Her face flamed and she bent hastily for her sherry glass.

'Well, I'm sorry you were all hurt, but so was I. I didn't reach my decision lightly.' And why, Kate thought with silent resentment, should I feel compelled to defend myself?

Lana's head was still bent over her glass. 'But it's always up to the woman, isn't it, to set the standards? First a man's mother, then his wife. If either of them fails him, he can go to pieces.'

Kate stood up. 'It's kind of you to be concerned, Lana, but this is something Michael and I must work out for ourselves.'

'And I've no right to interfere. I'm sorry. Let's change the subject. I believe Mr Mowbray's thinking of taking you with him next time he goes up north? I heard him discussing it with Mr Bailey.'

So that was it. Unattached, Kate loomed as a rival for Richard's attention. No wonder Lana wanted her safely back with Michael. Pitying her insecurity, Kate forgave her intrusion.

For the rest of the evening the conversation kept off the personal. On the surface at least, both women were relaxed and the time passed pleasantly. Lana left for her bus and Kate, mentally reviewing the evening, tidied up and washed the dishes. Perhaps she had been too quick to condemn Richard's treatment of Lana, since he'd been kind when she was in trouble. It was yet another shift in perception, another correction to her appraisal. How shallowly she must have judged them all.

Kate wrung out the dishcloth and draped it over the sink. She turned the lights out and had started towards the stairs, when the phone rang out in the darkened room. She hurried towards it, stumbling in her haste to reach it before its strident ringing woke Josh.

'Hello?'

Silence crawled along the wire, doubly sinister as she stood alone in the dark.

'Hello?' she repeated, trying to prevent her voice rising. 'Who is it? What do you want?'

Another pause, and then the impersonal click of the replaced receiver. Kate was trembling. Had someone been watching, waiting till Lana left and she was alone? Unlikely, this second time, for it to be a random call. She pulled back the curtain and looked out. The pavement below, fitfully illuminated by the sparsely spaced street lamps, was deserted. Across the expanse of the Green the Minster lay humped like a prehistoric monster in its lair. No one sat in the darkness on the wooden seats. And there wasn't a public phone box in sight.

Kate let the curtain fall, felt her way back across the room, and went up to bed.

CHAPTER 15

'*Broadshire Evening News* on the line for you, Guy.'

'Right. Put 'em through.' Webb pushed the pile of papers aside and leaned back in his chair. The phone crackled in his ear. 'Michael? What can I do for the gentlemen of the press?'

'Hello, Dave. Thought you'd like to know we've received a so-called confession to the murders.'

Webb grunted. 'Anonymous phone call?'

'No, a letter. Name and address supplied. He must want us to find him.'

'Have you done anything about it?'

'Not yet. I felt it was your pigeon. It was probably addressed to me because of that feature story I did.'

'Right. Let's have it, then.' He reached for a pad.

'Name of Riley, eleven, Milton Avenue, Bridgefield. It's that new estate off the Nailsworth road.'

'OK, we'll follow it up. Any lead's welcome at the moment.'

'If you want to collect it on your way, I'll leave it at reception.'

'Thanks, Mike. Cheers.' He replaced the phone and raised his voice. 'Ken! On your feet, lad. We're on our way to Shillingham.'

Saturday morning. Ten days now since the last murder, and still nothing concrete to go on, though a few clues were beginning to emerge, thanks to Forensic. Pine needles, for instance. Not much to go on, heaven knew, but traces of pine needles had been found at two of the four scenes of crime. And that was a puzzle in itself. Why only two? Had the murderer set out from different places?

Ken Jackson was driving. Webb settled back and closed his eyes, but the Sergeant knew it was not in relaxation. The Chief Inspector's mind would still be ticking over possible leads, dead ends, points to be clarified. In confirmation of his thoughts, Webb spoke suddenly without opening his eyes.

'Tell me, Ken, what the hell did we do with our time BD?'

'BD, Guy?'

'Before Delilah. There *was* such a time, I suppose.'

Webb heard the grin in the Sergeant's voice. 'Suppose there must have been, but I don't remember it myself.'

Saturday morning. Hannah'd be home, padding about the flat on her weekly chores, hair tied back with a bit of ribbon. So clear was his mental picture of her that he wished with brief vehemence that he could drop Jackson off and go to her, spend an idle day loafing about with regular toppings up of the coffee she made so well. The peace, the restfulness of her: that, more than her body, was what he craved at that moment.

He became aware that the car was stopping and opened his eyes. They were outside the offices of the *Broadshire News*.

'I'll just nip in and collect the billy-doo.' The way Jackson pronounced it made no spelling variant possible. Webb smiled, looking after the slight, hurrying figure. Who was he to complain? At least he had no wife patiently awaiting his non-arrival. Poor

Ken. He must be getting withdrawal symptoms for his plump, even-tempered Millie.

He held out his hand for the letter as Jackson climbed back into the car. 'Needn't bother about fingerprints, since we're on our way to see him.'

'The address was checked, I suppose?'

'I did it myself. An F. Riley does indeed live at eleven, Milton Avenue.' He glanced at the printed signature. 'Though this is from Maurice of that ilk.'

'What does he say?'

'"You can tell the coppers it was me that done the Delilahs, all four of them. Jolly good riddance too. Yrs truly, Maurice Riley."'

'Brief and to the point.'

'Semi-literate hand. So much for our educational system.'

They took the northwest road out of town and minutes later the ugly, uniform shapes of the council houses appeared on their left. Milton Avenue lay in the heart of the estate, and No. 11 was a small semi-detached house painted a vivid shade of turquoise. The grass at the front was rough and untended, looking, Jackson thought, as though it had been cut with nail scissors. Farther down the road some noisy little boys were charging up and down on bicycles, shouting to each other. Nearly every driveway boasted a car of some sort, and fifty percent of them were in the process of being washed.

With Jackson behind him, Webb strode up the path and pressed the bell. A peal of 'Jingle Bells' reached them and the door opened to reveal a boy of about seventeen. His long dark hair had received much the same treatment as the front grass, and his eyes, long-lashed and velvet brown, made Jackson think of cows. His mouth was full and sulky and he wore a soiled T-shirt and scruffy jeans.

'Ma's out,' he said without interest. 'Gone to Bingo. And Dad's at the pub.'

'Mr Maurice Riley?' Webb asked smoothly. The girlish eyes widened. 'Yeh?'

'Detective Chief Inspector Webb of Shillingham CID.' He held up his card. 'I'd like a word about the letter you sent to the *Broadshire News*.' He was watching the boy closely, analysing the expressions that crossed his face in rapid succession: initial panic, then gratification at the success of his ploy, and a swaggering bravado.

'Yeh?' He squared his narrow shoulders.

'Perhaps we could come inside?'

'Well—I suppose so, but Ma'll be back soon.'

Some murderer, Jackson thought disgustedly, afraid of his mother! The small front room was a study in beige. Three-piece suite, curtains, walls, and carpet were uncompromisingly the same. The room had a little-used air about it, not conducive to probing motives behind the letter-sending.

'I think we'd be more comfortable in your room,' Webb said decisively. 'Would you like to lead the way?'

Riley seemed taken aback. 'But it's not been tidied.'

'We won't worry about that.'

They followed him up the narrow staircase. Through the thin wall they could hear a baby crying next door. At the top of the stairs a door stood open showing a bathroom tiled in bright pink. A dirty towel lay crumpled on the floor.

The boy's room was the small front one over the porch. It contained an unmade bed, a chair weighed down with discarded clothing, and a chest of drawers on top of which stood a mug of cold tea, a lurid paperback, a transistor radio, and a bicycle lamp. Behind the chest a spotted mirror hung lopsidedly on the wall, the only other decoration being a dog-eared photograph of Elvis Presley torn from a magazine.

Webb seated himself at the foot of the bed, motioned Jackson to join him, and the Sergeant took out his pocket book.

'Right, Mr Riley. Now perhaps you'd like to make a statement.'

The boy licked his lips, eyes darting as though for reassurance round the familiar room. 'Don't I have to go to the nick for that?'

'Not in the first instance. Go ahead, please.'

'Well—I mean, I said it all, didn't I? In the letter.'

'You murdered these four women?'

Riley nodded, adding for emphasis, 'Like I said.'

'And how exactly did you go about it?'

'Well, I—went to their houses, like, and when they wasn't expecting it, I plunged the knife in.'

'What knife would that be, Mr Riley?'

'The bread knife. I took it with me.'

'I see. So you went along the road carrying a bread knife, rang the bell, and the victim unhesitatingly let you in?'

'Yes. I said I was a friend of her old man.'

'I see. Go on.'

'That's all. I told you.'

'But what did you do next?' Webb asked with heavy patience.

'I knifed her, didn't I? Then I walked out of the house and came home.'

'What about the writing on the mirror?'

'Oh yeh. I done that, and all.'

Webb produced a piece of paper from his pocket. 'Would you write here, please, exactly what you wrote on the mirrors?'

Riley hesitated. 'You seen it, didn't you?'

'Nevertheless, I'd like you to write it down.' He handed over his own pen. After a moment, in uncertain capitals, Riley wrote slowly 'Death to Dililha'.

'That's how you spelt it, is it?'

'I know there's an haitch somewhere.'

Webb pocketed paper and pen and rose to his feet. 'I take it you've no objection to our searching the room?'

For the first time, alarm showed on the boy's face. 'Yes. Yes, I have, as a matter of fact. You have to have a warrant for that.'

'Not if we've your permission. Otherwise, of course, we can always get one.'

'But it's—private like. I don't let no one in there.' His eyes were fastened anxiously on the chest of drawers.

'Mr Riley, you've made a confession of murder. You should have realized we'd search your belongings, and with or without a warrant, I intend to do so. Which is it to be?'

The boy muttered something and turned away.

'What was that?'

'All right, if you must. But them things are private.'

Jackson had already moved to the chest. There were four drawers in it, and by the time they reached the bottom one, Webb was wondering what the boy was so frightened of. Admittedly, there were some soft porn magazines of the type readily available at less reputable newsagents. Other than that, there were simply belts, sweaters, shirts, and a couple of combs black with dirt. But as Jackson reached for the last drawer Riley's tension was tangible and Webb could smell his sweat. He watched with interest as Jackson neatly and efficiently removed more shirts, another pair of jeans, some socks. At the back of the drawer, finally exposed, was a flat white box. From the corner of his eye, he could see Riley's clenched fists as he waited, not breathing, for his secret to be revealed. It had to be dope, Webb thought resignedly. Though the boy didn't look like an addict, it could be nothing else. He bent forward curiously as Jackson lifted the lid, and for a moment both men stared uncomprehendingly at the contents. Then, with a blank face, Jackson lifted them out one by one and laid them on the dingy carpet. A transparent black nightdress in cheap nylon, a brassiere, a pair of French knickers, a suspender belt and a pair of stockings. And last of all, in the back corner, a tube of lipstick and some mascara.

'Your girlfriend's?' Webb asked expressionlessly, but he knew the answer.

Riley's face was wretched. 'If Ma found out—'

'Are they stolen property?'

'No—no, they're not. Honest. I bought them out of my wages. Said they were for my sister.'

'But they weren't?'

Riley hung his head and Webb felt a stab of pity. 'When do you wear them?'

'When they're all out. I dress up, like. It doesn't do no harm, does it?' He was miserably defiant.

'Not as much as murdering people.'

'Yeh. Well, I was having you on there.'

'You withdraw your statement?'

'I suppose so, yes.'

'You realize there are penalties for wasting police time?'

Riley licked his lips again. 'I'm sorry, mister. I didn't mean no harm.' He paused. It was clear which anxiety was uppermost in his mind. 'You won't tell Ma, will you? Honest to God I didn't nick 'em, I swear it.'

Webb's eyes moved over the pretty face, shining now with perspiration. There was unlikely to be any more trouble from this source.

'As you say, Mr Riley, dressing up doesn't hurt anyone. We're more concerned with the making of false claims and wasting our time. However, for the moment we'll take no further action.'

Back in the car Jackson said unbelievingly, 'What do you make of that? He'd rather be thought a murderer than a transvestite!'

'One of nature's accidents,' Webb commented.

'Odd about the spelling, too. He got it right in the letter.'

'Probably copied it from the paper the first time.'

They emerged onto the main road and Jackson turned the car in the direction of Shillingham. 'One consolation, anyway,' he said gloomily, 'we didn't expect to get anywhere on this one.'

The Chief Inspector did not reply.

'Interested in classical music, Kate?'

Kate looked up from the invoice she was studying. 'Of the lighter kind, yes I am.' 'How do Bruch and Vivaldi grab you?'

'Two of my favourites. Why?'

'Naomi Fairchild's playing at the Southern Hall. I wondered if you'd like to go along.'

Kate's eyes flew to Lana who, with compressed lips, embarked on a machine-gun rattle of typing.

'I—don't see how I can, Richard.'

'Why not? Lana'd babysit, wouldn't you, my love?'

Lana said stiffly, 'I'm already sitting for Mrs Romilly on Thursday. I'm afraid that's my only free evening.'

Kate said in a rush, 'I really think we'd better leave it, Richard. As Lana said, I'm going to the school on Thursday, and—'

'Nonsense. Nella'll come if you ask her. Since you're booked for Thursday and I'm out tomorrow, we'd better make it Wednesday. We can have something to eat first.'

Kate knew she wanted to go. Enigmatic and infuriating though Richard could be, she was increasingly attracted to him: in direct relation, she admitted, to Michael's steady withdrawal. And it was Michael who'd insisted they regard themselves as free during this period; advice which he was undoubtedly following himself.

Richard had reached across Lana and pulled the phone towards him. 'Nella? Could you be a lamb and sit for Kate on Wednesday while I entertain her?... What time would that be?... Oh, no problem, then. We'd be back by then. Bless you, my love.'

Did he call every woman his love? Kate wondered on an upsurge of irritability. Richard said easily, 'That's settled. She's going to supper with a mob of photographers, but as they're meeting in the pub they won't move till closing time. I told her we'll be back in time to release her.'

Kate wondered if Martin were included in the jollifications. He was still subdued after his confession and had been keeping out of her way.

'Incidentally, Kate,' Richard added, 'I'd be grateful if you'd do something for me. I bought some etchings yesterday from a woman in Beaumont Crescent, but I hadn't the car with me. Could you pop in this afternoon and collect them? It's a Mrs

Rammage at number twenty-two. Martin will be here to keep an eye on things.'

Kate hadn't done errands for the shop before, and she enjoyed the break in routine. Beaumont Crescent was in a wealthy part of town, the houses solid and well maintained, the road lined with trees. There had been a wind during the night and shoals of leaves, crisp and golden, whirled desultorily in the gutters.

A pretty French girl, presumably an *au pair*, opened the door to Kate and handed over the unwieldy parcel. Kate drove slowly back to Monks' Walk, supposedly to protect her cargo but in fact to prolong the outing. She parked briefly outside Pennyfarthings, where Martin came out to relieve her of the parcel, and then made her way back to her parking space in Lady Ann Square. The sky overhead was wide and blue, the sun mellow. It was, she thought ruefully, the day for a brisk country walk rather than being shut up indoors.

She was aware of voices as she got out of the car and found they were coming from behind the wall immediately in front of her. But it was only as she turned from locking the car that, with a shock of surprise, she identified them. They belonged to Paul and Sylvia. Bewildered, Kate paused to get her bearings, and realized for the first time that the Danes' garden must back onto the square. From the closeness of their voices, Paul and Sylvia were just the other side of the wall.

'You mean to tell me,' Sylvia was saying laughingly, 'that after my bringing you all the way down here, you won't accept it?'

'My dear, how could I explain a rose in my buttonhole? I'm supposed to be spending my free period in the library. And think of the grilling I'd get from Madge!'

Sylvia's low laugh. 'You're getting quite neurotic about these little visits, darling! And she'll know soon enough.'

'Not till the time is ripe.'

With an effort Kate forced herself to walk out of the square. Her eavesdropping was unintentional. When she'd first recognized the voices, she'd been incapable for several seconds of moving away. Now, uselessly, she wished she had. What did they mean, Madge would know soon enough? Surely they weren't serious about each other? According to gossip, Sylvia's many intrigues were puffball affairs. Their only saving grace was that no one had been hurt by them. Twice before, Kate had argued herself out of suspicions of Paul, but the words she'd overheard nullified the excuses she'd thought up on his behalf. And there was nothing she could do. Knowledge of her helplessness intensified her despair.

The next morning, Josh, unusually, was ready before Kate. 'Come on, Mum, we'll be late,' he urged for the second time. Kate smudged her lipstick and swore softly.

'Wait downstairs, Josh, for goodness sake. Go and see if your comic's arrived.'

He clattered off down the stairs and Kate completed her toilet in peace. It was as she started after him that she heard the sounds, a choked cry followed by a thud and a soft, muted scream. Then, almost simultaneously, Lana's voice.

'Josh, is that you? What—? Oh my God!'

Kate hurtled round the bend in the stairs and stopped aghast. Josh, ashen-faced, was standing in the passage staring at something that lay on the floor. Kate couldn't see what it was because Lana, pulling the child's stiffly resisting body against her, was blocking the view.

'Josh?' Kate ran down the last few steps. 'Darling, whatever—?'

'I'm going to be sick,' he announced indistinctly.

'I'll take him.' Swiftly Lana pushed him in front of her into the office and through to the tiny cloakroom the other side, leaving Kate staring down at the pieces of dead mouse scattered over the floor. Oh no! she thought numbly, not again! The sound of Josh's vomiting galvanized her into action. She ran to him, unceremoniously pushing Lana aside, and held his forehead. 'There, darling, it's all right, it's all right.'

'I don't—understand,' he said between shuddering gasps. 'What was it doing in the little box? Was it supposed to be for me?'

'I don't know, darling. Just some silly joke. Don't worry about it.'

'But it was—pulled apart.' He retched again and Kate's own throat closed in sympathy.

Martin's voice now, in the office behind her. 'What the hell's going on?' And Lana's unsteady murmured reply.

'Ye gods! Where did it come from?'

Kate said over her shoulder, 'Martin—'

'Of course. I'll get a shovel.'

She didn't consider where he'd find such a thing. She was only concerned with getting Josh away from the scene as swiftly as possible.

'You'll be late for school, darling, come along.' Much better to have his mind immediately taken off the incident. 'All right? You mustn't let it upset you. Someone was being very stupid and—and the mouse wouldn't have known anything about it.' Please God.

He nodded, wiped his hand across his mouth, and straightened up. She led him through the shop and out of the front door, amazed that her legs should support her. Madge and Tim were waiting in the usual place.

Kate said rapidly, 'Josh has just had an unpleasant shock. Nothing serious, but I'll tell you about it later.'

'Is he all right?' Madge looked with concern at the child's white face, his eyes still red-rimmed from retching.

'He will be. I must get back, Madge.'

'Anything I can do?'

Kate shook her head and started back to the shop. Richard had arrived in her absence. He came quickly forward and drew her towards him. 'Are you all right, Kate?'

'Yes, I think so.'

'I can't get any sense out of Lana, and Martin apparently wasn't here—'

'Something—was left in the letter box.'

'A dismembered mouse?' Richard's voice rose with incredulity.

'It's happened before. Last time it was a moth.'

'Then it's high time the police heard about it.'

'No.' Kate shook her head. 'It's all right, Richard. I think I know who's doing it and they're not—dangerous or anything.'

'Who, then?' He tipped her head back, staring frowningly down at her. She noted dispassionately that there were gold flecks in the hazel of his eyes.

'Some boys Josh and I met one night. They followed us home.'

'That's no reason why they shouldn't be stopped from pestering you.'

'But I don't know who they are,' Kate said with careful reason. 'Please, Richard, much the best thing is just to ignore it.'

'Well, if you say so, and you really are all right.'

He bent his head and absentmindedly kissed her. Except

that nothing Richard did was absentminded. It was a brief kiss, exerting a minimum pressure and almost immediately withdrawn. Passionless, merely comforting. His eyes when she raised hers to meet them were veiled, uncommunicative.

'Better?'

She nodded and, still with his arm round her, he led her into the office. Lana sat tremblingly at her desk, a glass of water beside her. Martin was washing his hands in the cloakroom.

'OK,' he said briskly. 'All over and done with. Except for this.' He indicated a small cardboard box, similar to the one in which the moth had been delivered. On the lid was written in black letters 'For the lady upstairs'.

'Too bad Josh had to open it,' Martin added. 'It would have been bad enough for Kate.'

'He didn't see the writing,' Lana said. 'He had it upside down, that's why it fell on the floor. Oh God!' She put both hands to her mouth. 'His little face!'

Richard said, 'Kate doesn't want us to do anything. Against my advice, but it's up to her. She thinks it came from some boys who followed her the other night.'

'And chalked up a word on your door?'

Kate nodded. 'It's all very childish but I suppose it amuses them. Thank you all for helping.'

'Then perhaps if order is restored, we can now open for business.'

Madge phoned shortly afterwards, anxious to know the cause of the upset, but Kate made light of it. Her suspicion of Paul had effectively closed off his home as her bolthole and place of comfort. Madge knew her too well for Kate to be able to conceal her changed attitude towards him.

Josh was still pale when he returned from school and Kate noted achingly that he averted his eyes from the passage floor. With luck he'd soon forget, but he was a sensitive child and fond of animals. At best, he'd had an extremely unpleasant experience.

It resurrected itself that night. Kate was reading when he suddenly started to scream. She rushed upstairs to find him sitting up in bed, eyes wide open and pyjamas wringing wet. It took her a long time to soothe him, even longer before he'd let her leave the room. Unless he was better the next day, it would be impossible for her to go to the concert.

When she returned downstairs, Kate felt in need of comfort herself and, reaching a swift decision, went to the phone and dialled Michael's number. He still had Josh's interests at heart. The phone rang for a long time and she was about to give up when the ringing abruptly ceased and a girl's voice said breathlessly, 'Hello?'

Kate stiffened, her hand tightening on the phone. Then, like her own tormentor, she replaced it without a word.

By the next morning Josh at least had recovered his equilibrium, though he was careful to wait for his mother before venturing downstairs. All being well, she'd get to the concert after all.

Nella arrived with Richard at six-thirty. Dressed, Kate presumed, for a late informal supper, she sported a cowl-necked sweater in canary yellow, skin-tight jeans, green leg-warmers, and ankle boots in purple suede. As always, she looked delectable.

The restaurant Richard had chosen for their early meal was small and intimate, almost deserted at that hour of the evening. The lights were shaded and candles flickered on the tables. Kate thought suddenly, 'It's like a scene from TV, the prelude to a seduction!', and then caught her breath. Perhaps that's what it was.

But if Richard had plans, he was not revealing them yet. Throughout the meal and the concert that followed he was polite, formal, and completely impersonal, as though they were strangers meeting for the first time. Kate hadn't known what she expected of the evening, but it was not this. To her shame, she was aware of baffled disappointment.

They emerged from the concert hall at nine-thirty. 'It's early to end the evening,' Richard commented as they walked to the car, 'but we promised Nella to go straight back. Perhaps we could have coffee at the flat.'

Guiltily Kate remembered Josh and wondered if he'd woken and needed her. Nella put her mind at rest.

'Not a dicky-bird!' she told them cheerfully, packing away some surprisingly intricate embroidery she had brought with her. 'He was so quiet I went up once to have a look at him. He was sound asleep.'

Richard saw Nella out while Kate went to make coffee. When she carried it through, Richard was leafing through a library book she'd left on the table. He looked up, watching her move towards him, and her pulses started racing. This, then, was what the evening had been building towards. She was not mistaken after all.

She put the tray on the table and bent to pour the coffee, but his hand stopped her.

'Leave that for a moment,' he said, turning her to face him. He was the exact opposite of Michael, Kate thought incoherently, stocky where her husband was thin and wiry, hair thick and straight instead of dark and crinkly. Only the expression in his eyes was the same, and her starved body responded to it in the self-same way.

It was some moments before the first doubts came and she turned her head away. His open mouth moved over her neck and ear and she shuddered under its caress, trying above the clamour of her body to define the unwelcome mental reservations. He said softly, 'Last time we were here together, you were in your nightdress. Shall we take it from there?' She caught her breath and he went on more urgently, 'We're not schoolchildren, Kate. We both know what we want and there'll never be a better time. You're in need of therapy—let's apply it now.'

But the doubts had crystallized and Kate knew with despairing resentment that her loyalties were still with Michael. Ten years of his lovemaking, familiar and tender, still outweighed the promised excitement of Richard's. It was unfair, but there was no escaping it.

He had been watching her tensely and now dropped his hands with a short laugh. 'The answer's no, isn't it? Well, it was worth a try. No hard feelings.'

'I'm—sorry,' Kate murmured, and bent to the coffee tray. Damn Michael! she thought with sudden vehemence. Damn him for keeping her in thrall after shrugging off her own claims.

Her hands were still shaking as she passed Richard his coffee.

CHAPTER 16

After Richard had gone, Kate sat for a long time in the silent room, waiting for her jumping nerves to settle. On the table in front of her the tray still stood with their empty cups. The smell of cold coffee titillated her nostrils, overlaid by a memory of Nella's scent from earlier in the evening. Kate imagined her now, vivid and full of life, talking and laughing with her friends. Nella, Richard, Martin, Lana. They were so much a part of her life that it was startling to realize how little she knew them. And of them all only Nella, flamboyant and outrageous, had been completely open with her. The others, for reasons of their own, kept her at a distance.

She tried to think of them objectively; Martin, whose ready smile masked a furtiveness she hadn't at first suspected; Lana, reserved and wary, jealous of Richard's attention; and Richard himself, acknowledging his desire but remaining cool and uninformative to the point of anonymity.

Yet in this new and hostile world they were all she had. Madge, tried friend of many years, was barred to her now by Paul's deception. Nor could she approach Michael. At the weekend they'd exchanged barely a dozen words, and a telephone call might be answered by Jill.

Essentially she was alone, and in her aloneness the pinpricks of unease occasioned by the moth, the mouse, the silent phone calls, escalated into a menace she could no longer dismiss as chance. For some reason she was being deliberately singled out for harassment. Why?

Her mind switched with terrifying logic to the Delilah victims. Had their final retribution come on the same unanswered question? Kate went cold. Suppose they too had received prior, unexplained warning of their fate?

She stood up abruptly, knocking against the low table so that the cups rattled. Tomorrow she'd tell Richard the whole story. He'd been concerned for her about the mouse, he'd be able to advise her.

The relief at the prospect of transferring her burden was immense, and on the crest of it she went to bed.

But her peace of mind was tempered by the dream she had that night. In it, she was clinging to a cliff face while below her the incoming tide rushed into a rocky cove. Gulls circled overhead screaming discordantly, but above their cry she heard her name called and, looking up, saw Richard leaning over the cliff top.

Painfully she inched her way up, sliding and scrabbling with bleeding hands until, at the limit of her endurance, her stretching fingers touched his. And suddenly, shockingly, he wrenched himself free, prising her fingers from his to send her hurtling away to fall, spiralling crazily, to the dark and jagged sea below. As she fell she heard herself crying out his name in a long, despairing scream.

It was the scream that woke her, shuddering and sweating,

and not even the reassuring light she reached for could dispel the strands of nightmare. Because, hidden in the melodrama, was a grain of truth. Despite Richard's caresses, she had no idea whether or not she could trust him.

The effect of the dream survived the night, remaining with Kate and colouring everything with nebulous uncertainty.

'How's Josh?' Lana inquired over coffee.

'He's not had any more nightmares.' Last night, it had been her turn.

'Poor little soul, I felt so sorry for him.'

'You must have an admirer, Kate,' said Martin. 'Count Dracula, perhaps.'

Kate forced a smile and did not reply.

Though she'd been apprehensive of seeing Richard again, he gave no hint of embarrassment. It was as though he'd never held her, never urged her to make love to him. The incident seemed as unreal as his image in her dream, and it struck her that even if they had spent the night together his attitude would not have changed. It was a humiliating thought.

At twelve-thirty Lana asked what time she'd be required that evening, and Kate, who'd forgotten it was parents' evening, hastily collected herself.

'About seven if you can manage it, Lana. We're asked to be there by a quarter past.'

Josh returned from school with the information that Madge would wait for Kate on the usual corner. 'Uncle Paul isn't going,' he added. 'He's got a sore throat so he wasn't at school today.'

Guiltily, Kate was grateful. She had no wish to come face to face with Paul.

'I hope Josh won't wake while you're out,' Lana said on arrival. 'If he was frightened, it would be you he'd want.'

'I think he's over it now,' Kate reassured her. All the same, Josh hadn't recovered his normal *joie-de-vivre*. She hoped he wasn't about to go down with the whooping cough Paul had mentioned.

There would be rain later, Kate thought as she pulled the door shut behind her. Heavy purple clouds were banking to the east and against them the outlines of roofs and trees were stencilled with abnormal clarity. It gave to the scene an ominous sense of importance, almost of foreboding, like a stage set for tragedy. She shook herself and hurried on, thinking more prosaically that she should have brought an umbrella.

Catching sight of Madge on the corner, Kate felt a rush of affection. Damn Paul for coming between them! She threaded her arm impulsively through Madge's and gave it a little squeeze. Madge's slightly anxious look disappeared.

'That's better!' she commented. 'I was getting worried about you. You almost seem to have been avoiding me.'

'Nonsense!' Kate said roundly. 'You won't get rid of me as easily as that!'

The hall was crowded as they took their seats on the under-sized chairs that are the penance of parents' evenings the world over. 'I'm sorry Paul isn't well,' Kate said dutifully.

'A touch of tonsillitis, I think. The doctor's put him on anti-biotics but he's not in bed.'

Kate hoped darkly that, with Madge and Henry safely occupied, he would not take the chance of slipping round to Sylvia's. She might be prepared to risk a sore throat in the furtherance of their affair.

'At least,' Madge was adding, 'it saved the bother of finding a babysitter.' And Kate relaxed. Paul was unlikely to abandon his children, even if his wife was not afforded such consideration.

The Headmaster, resplendent in cap and gown, took his place on the platform and the evening began with a speech outlining the policies and achievements of the school. Afterwards, the parents scattered to seek out those masters who taught their own sons.

'There's no point in waiting for each other,' Madge told Kate. 'One of us is bound to finish before the other. But come round after work tomorrow and we'll have a cup of tea. I haven't seen much of you lately.'

Unhappily, Kate knew she'd make an excuse. Paul was home and not confined to bed. She didn't want him present at their chat.

She forgot her regrets for the next hour or so as she learned with pleasure of the progress her son was making. He had settled in with no problems and adapted to the increased volume of work. Master after master confirmed Henry's earlier opinion of Josh's abilities, and it was with Henry himself that Kate ended her round.

As she sat down at his desk, he gave an exclamation of annoyance. 'How stupid of me! I put out that book of poetry to bring this evening, and came away without it. I do apologize.'

Kate assured him it didn't matter, but when she left him minutes later, he urged her to call in for the book on the way home. 'You'll be passing the door, and Sylvia will give it to you. It's on the hall table, tell her.'

To please him, Kate promised she would, though she was no more eager to see Sylvia than Paul. Still, it would hurt Henry if she didn't call, and she needn't go in. Lana's bus provided an excellent excuse for going straight on home.

The rain which had been foreshadowed earlier was falling heavily as Kate left the school. Street lamps shone on glistening pavements and parents leaving with her made quick dashes for their cars. In the headlights the rain glanced down diagonally like showers of silver arrows. Kate turned up the collar of her coat, dug her hands deep into her pockets, and set off briskly down the road, avoiding the rushing passage of cars which sent a spray of mud across the pavements. She was glad when she could turn off the busy thoroughfare of Broad Street into the quietness of Monks' Walk.

She was almost tempted to go back on her promise and give Sylvia's house a miss. Henry'd understand, in view of the weather and her lack of umbrella. But it was, after all, on her way, and he'd been kind enough to find the book for her.

With a sigh, Kate turned into the gateway and hurried up the path. Light showed behind the drawn sitting room curtains and the frosted panel in the front door. She pressed the bell and waited, listening to the steady patter of rain on the path behind her. It was encouraging that Josh was doing so well; Michael would be pleased to hear of his progress. For the first time she wondered if she should have told him in advance about this evening. Still, they couldn't have gone together in the circumstances.

Oh, come *on*, Sylvia! Kate pressed the bell again, glancing at her watch in the uncertain light. It was only nine-thirty and Lana would not yet be worrying about her bus. All the same, Kate was herself cold and wet and longing to be home. On a wave of impatience she turned the handle and to her surprise the door swung inwards.

A smell of curry prickled her nose. Ahead of her stretched

the remembered hall, and on the oak table just inside lay the book of poetry. Kate was tempted simply to take it and go.

'Hello?' she called. 'Sylvia? Henry asked me to collect the book.'

There was silence. Not even the sound of television to explain Sylvia's non-appearance. Perhaps she was having a bath?

'Hello?' she called again. Pushing the front door shut, she crossed the hall and tapped at the sitting room door, turning the handle as she did so. Sylvia was sitting with her back to the door. She must be asleep.

'Sylvia, it's Kate. Sorry to disturb you, but—' Her voice trailed off as she moved round the chair and experienced a jolt when she saw the woman's eyes were open.

'What is it?' she said sharply. 'Are you ill?' She bent forward, touching one of her hands. It slid sideways off her lap and very slowly Kate backed away, staring down at her. A stroke? she thought agitatedly. A heart attack? Should she feel for a pulse? Sylvia's white blouse was spotted with red. Gradually, unwillingly, Kate was realizing that the spots weren't evenly spaced. This can't be happening, thought part of her brain, but with magnetic dread her eyes were drawn to the shadows above the lamplight, where the antique mirror hung over the fireplace. And there was no surprise in what she saw there.

She thought clearly, Henry'll be back soon. He mustn't find her like this. A slight movement from Sylvia's direction caught her eye, and with wild unreasoning hope she spun round. But it was only a fly and to her unspeakable horror it settled on one of the exposed eyeballs and proceeded to clean its legs.

Kate felt the bile rush into her throat. She stumbled out of the room, all coherency fled, clawed at the front door and, leaving it open, blundered down the path and out onto the pavement. Immediately she collided with someone—someone who caught hold of her and exclaimed, 'Kate—is it you? What's wrong?' It was Richard.

She raised her wild face to his. 'Sylvia's dead—murdered. I've just seen her.' She swayed and he steadied her.

'Mrs Dane? You're sure?'

'Oh, I'm sure. And there's lipstick on the mirror. Richard, we must stop Henry—'

'Have you phoned the police? Kate?' He shook her as she broke into despairing sobs.

'No, I couldn't stay there. Oh God, Richard—*there was a fly on her eye!*' She retched and again he held her, waiting for the spasm to pass.

'We must phone straightaway. Come on, I'll come back with you.' And at her frenzied resistance: 'You needn't see her again, I promise.' He hurried her back up the path and through the open front door. Kate averted her eyes from the sitting room and Richard led her quickly past it to the kitchen.

'Sit here for a minute while I phone the police. And I'd better make certain she's dead.'

Kate sat unmoving for long minutes while, despite her assurances, Richard went to check the dead woman. Then she heard his voice briefly on the phone. He came back into the kitchen folding his handkerchief and, seeing her glance, smiled self-consciously.

'Perhaps I read too many thrillers, but I thought it best not to touch anything. We have to stay here till the police arrive, but they won't be long. God, what a business.'

She wasn't sure if she was trembling or shivering, but rain ran off her hair inside her collar and her hands were like ice. Richard took them between his own and began to massage them.

'We must stop Henry,' she moaned.

'The police will see to that. They'll be here any minute.' There was an air of suppressed excitement about him, as though he welcomed the challenge to his initiative, the need to remain calm in a crisis. He seemed almost disappointed when, after a preliminary ring, the front door opened and Constable Timms hurried in.

Richard, still holding Kate's hands, nodded towards the sitting room and the constable disappeared inside. A moment later he reappeared.

'Right, sir. Have either you or the young lady touched anything?'

'I haven't. The front door was open and I used a handkerchief for the phone. I'm not sure about Kate. She found her.'

Constable Timms bent down. 'Are you all right, ma'am?' Before, at the shop, she had thought him a rather pompous young man. Now he was in charge, solid, dependable, the embodiment of law and order.

'Can you remember if you touched anything?'

Her lips felt like rubber. 'I opened the front door when no one answered the bell. 'And I'—she gasped—'I touched her hand.'

'Was it cold?' Richard asked, and Timms glanced at him reprovingly.

'No,' Kate answered mechanically, 'quite normal. Oh God!' She caught her lip between her teeth and added piteously, 'I've never seen anyone dead before.'

'Can I take her home, Constable? She's in a state of shock.'

'I'm afraid you'll have to wait for the investigating officer, sir. He shouldn't be long.'

They arrived almost together, Webb, Stapleton the pathologist, and the police doctor, but they did not come to the kitchen. Kate continued to sit there,

Richard was silent at her side. She had stopped feeling cold, feeling anything, in fact, till sensation returned in full measure with the awareness of something brushing against her legs. With a gasping shriek she jumped from the chair, sending it skidding across the floor as a small form shot from under the table and out of the door. It was the grey cat Madge had stroked at the dinner party.

Kate gazed after it, waiting for the clattering of her heart to subside.

'Pity it can't talk,' Richard commented, righting her chair. 'It might have saved everyone a lot of trouble.'

They both turned as Webb came into the room. 'I'm sorry to keep you waiting. Do sit down. Chief Inspector Webb of Shillingham CID. Mrs Romilly and Mr Mowbray, is that right?' He glanced at Kate. 'Any connection with Michael Romilly of the *Broadshire News*?'

'He's my husband,' she said dully.

'I wondered. Unusual name. And you found the body, I believe. Are you feeling a little better now?'

'Not much.'

'We'll get the police doctor to look at you before we take a full statement, but I'm afraid there are some questions that can't wait. I'd like you to tell me exactly what happened, why you came to the house and so on.'

'I'd been to the school—parents' evening. Mr Dane asked me to collect a book on my way home.'

'The front door was open?'

'No, but it wasn't locked. When Sylvia didn't answer I tried the handle.'

'Go on.'

The shaking started again. Richard said roughly, 'Can't you let her go? She's in shock, for God's sake. She'll tell you everything in the morning.'

'I'm sorry, sir. The doctor will see her in a moment, but the first account is vital, while it's still fresh. Memory can play funny tricks, especially in cases of shock.' All the same, he'd have to check she was fit to be questioned. Her hands were spread-eagled on her cheeks and above them her eyes, a deep blue-black, stared at him unseeingly. Webb wished he could lean forward and gently draw her hands from her face.

Kate said for the third time, 'Please don't let Henry see her.'

'It's all right, Mrs Romilly,' Webb assured her. 'Someone's been sent to the school. He'll know by now what's happened.'

He was gentle and patient with her, but he let her omit nothing. The staring eyes with their expression of blank surprise, the lifeless hand, the fly, the scrawl on the mirror, all had to be described, lived through again. Suddenly, as though coming back to life,

Kate jerked upright. 'I must get home! Lana will miss her bus!'

'Miss Truscott's baby-sitting,' Richard explained. 'She lives in Littlemarsh.'

'Truscott? I know that name. Pulled a chap out of the river about six months ago.' 'Her brother,' said Richard briefly.

'Well, we'll get someone to run her home.'

'But she won't know that,' Kate insisted, 'she'll be worrying—and Josh might have woken. I must go.'

'Very well, Mrs Romilly. I'll ask Dr Roscoe to look at you

and then you can go home. If the doctor gives the all-clear I'll be along in about half an hour to fill in more details.'

'I'll take her back,' Richard said firmly, getting to his feet.

'That won't be necessary, sir, but perhaps you'd be good enough to go down to the station with Sergeant Collins. We'll need a full statement from you as well. Don't worry about Mrs Romilly, a woman police officer will look after her.'

Ten minutes later, having seen the doctor, Kate was helped into the back of a police car by a woman detective. The rain was still streaming down. She had lost sight of Richard, and in this strange new world she missed him. He was her only link with normality.

Lana came hurrying down the stairs, her eyes widening at the sight of Kate's escort.

'You're very late, Kate. Has anything happened?'

'It's Sylvia,' Kate said jerkily, 'she's been murdered.'

'Sylvia? You mean Mrs Dane, the artist? But she lives quite near, doesn't she?'

'Mrs Romilly's a little shocked,' Detective-Constable Lucas put in smoothly. 'It was she who discovered the body.'

Lana gasped. 'But how could you? You were at the school!' Her eyes went uncomprehendingly from the policewoman to Kate. Then she said quickly, 'Look, I wish I could stay with you, but the bus—'

'Constable Ridley will run you home, miss. The car's waiting outside.'

Lana stared at her blankly. 'But there's no need. I—'

'You'll have missed the bus by now anyway. Ten-thirty, wasn't it?'

It was true, Kate realized, checking with her watch. Lana had no hope of reaching the bus station by ten-thirty. She seemed to realize this and, her immediate problem solved, turned back to Kate.

'Then would you like me to stay a while?'

'I'll be with her, miss. Probably all night. Don't worry.'

'They sent Richard to the police station,' Kate said.

'Mr Mowbray?' Lana's tone sharpened. 'How does he come into this?'

'I met him. He came back with me.'

The policewoman interrupted. 'If you don't mind, miss, your driver's waiting and I think Mrs Romilly should go and sit down.'

Kate said, 'Did Josh wake?'

Lana shook her head.

'Thank you for coming, Lana.'

The staircase had never seemed so long. Kate allowed herself to be helped up, her dripping coat finally removed, and settled by the hastily lit gas fire. Vaguely she was aware of movements behind her as the young woman made tea, but exhaustion was heavy on her eyelids. She hadn't slept well the previous night. Perhaps they'd let her sleep before she had to answer any more questions.

Her last conscious thought was that she hadn't collected the poetry book after all.

CHAPTER 17

She was a pretty little thing, Mrs Romilly. Webb couldn't imagine what she was doing here, with Michael presumably still in Shillingham. Another marriage breaking up? He sighed.

'Now, Mrs Romilly,' he began, disguising his weariness, 'let's go through it again, shall we? And this time Sergeant Jackson here will write it all down.'

She seemed a little calmer now, in her own surroundings. If chance allowed, he always preferred to conduct interviews, with suspects and witnesses alike, in their own homes rather than the police station. An inveterate absorber of atmosphere, he owed the solution of many of his cases to a supposedly relaxed half hour in someone's home.

Webb studied the young woman opposite. Her rain-soaked hair had dried in a soft halo of curls and her huge dark-blue eyes stood out in the pallor of her face. Beside her, Mary Lucas looked indecently robust and healthy.

'Right, now, first things first. Katherine Louise Romilly, I think you said. And would this be your permanent address?' His tone was bland but he watched her closely and caught the faint flush.

'I'm not sure.' Her voice was very low.

'Then we'd better have the other one too.'

'Treetops, Lethbridge Drive, Shillingham.'

The routine questions of date and place of birth she answered promptly, but a return of tension was apparent when he reverted to more pertinent matters.

'Can you tell me, Mrs Romilly, how well you knew the deceased?'

'Hardly at all, really. I did go to dinner once, with some friends.'

Dates and names were duly noted by the unobtrusive sergeant at the table.

'And when did you last see her alive?'

Kate looked confused. 'That was probably the last time.' In the kitchen, her head close to Paul's. Paul!

'Yes, Mrs Romilly? You've remembered something?'

'No.' She moistened her lips. 'I'm sure that was the last time.'

'But you've seen her husband since?'

'Only this evening, at school.'

'Tell me again about the book you went to collect.'

Was he trying to trip her up? Kate wondered in a panic. She recalled hearing somewhere that people who found bodies were sometimes suspected themselves. But he couldn't think—

Stumblingly she went through it all again: Henry's promise to lend her the book, her reluctance to stop off because of the rain. Again, some slight inflection must have betrayed her.

'That was your only reason for not wanting to call?'

'I—well, yes. Except that I was in a hurry to get home and relieve Miss Truscott.'

'But there was no urgency about that, was there? There was

more than an hour before Miss Truscott's bus was due. If you'd wanted, you even had time for a coffee with Mrs Dane.'

'I—didn't know her very well.'

'Or like her very much?' probed the Chief Inspector astutely. Kate caught her breath. 'She was always very pleasant to me.'

'What were the other occasions on which you'd met her?'

'At Mrs Netherby's one afternoon. That was the first time.'

'And?'

'She came to the shop once or twice.'

'Didn't she also attend your art exhibition?'

'Oh yes, the private view. I'd forgotten that.'

It had been a surprise to Webb to realize who the deceased was. A frequenter of art galleries in his spare moments, he had seen and admired examples of her work. No doubt, he thought sardonically, their prices would now rocket.

'And at the time of her death you were at St Benedict's School?'

Kate said very carefully, 'I don't know the time of her death.'

'A preliminary estimate gives it as between eight and eight-thirty this evening.'

'Then I was at the school, yes.'

'And that can be verified?'

She showed a brief flair of spirit. 'Certainly, by about six different masters. I didn't have any gaps between appointments.'

And so it went on in minute, to Kate obsessive, detail. She had one moment of panic; Webb asked if she knew of anyone visiting Sylvia recently. She could not, positively not, implicate Paul.

'You'll be interviewing all her friends, surely, everyone who knew her?'

'Of course, but any help you can give us—'

'I'm afraid I can't, not on that point.' She waited, not

breathing, for him to probe further, but though Webb noticed her tension he let it go.

The telephone shrilled, making them all jump. Sergeant Jackson reached out and lifted it, then looked at Webb.

'Mr Romilly, sir. He wants to speak to his wife.'

Kate didn't wait for Webb's nod. She said, 'Michael!' on an indrawn breath and ran to the phone.

'Kate? My God, are you all right? What in heaven's name happened?'

Her eyes swam with tears and she closed them, tipping the large drops down her cheeks. 'Oh, Michael,' she whispered.

'Shall I come straight down? I could be there in forty minutes.'

A picture of Jill floated across Kate's mind and she steadied herself. 'No, I'm all right. The police are here.' He'd know that, of course. She added in a rush, 'But if you could come tomorrow—'

'Will someone stay overnight?'

'I think so, yes.'

'Right. I'll be there first thing. Try to get some sleep, darling.'

Sergeant Jackson took the phone from her. The endearment was automatic, she was thinking. He probably didn't realize he'd said it. Thankfully she saw the Chief Inspector was on his feet.

'Right, Mrs Romilly, we'll leave you now to get some sleep. Miss Lucas will stay with you. She'll be quite comfortable on the sofa if you can spare a blanket.'

Kate looked helplessly about her. 'There must be one somewhere.'

Webb nodded to Jackson and the two men took their leave. Mary Lucas regarded Kate sympathetically. 'Did the doctor give you something to help you sleep?'

'Yes. It's here.' Kate fumbled in her handbag and produced a small white envelope containing a couple of tablets. 'I'd better take them now.'

She moved as though she were asleep already, the policewoman thought as Kate went to the kitchen. The tea caddy had been put back on the wrong shelf and she mechanically replaced it.

'Your little boy's a sound sleeper,' Mary said with a smile as she accompanied Kate upstairs in search of a blanket. Together they peeped into Josh's room. The child lay on his back, arms flung above his head, quilt on the floor. Kate went in softly and replaced it, her hand hovering above his forehead as though, Mary thought, longing to touch him but afraid of waking him. Pity the husband wasn't here when the poor woman needed him.

The necessary blanket having been located, Mary retreated. Kate was alone for the first time since she had come hurtling out of the Danes' house three long hours before. Fumblingly, she started to undress.

The Minster clock was chiming a quarter to nine as Michael leant on the bell. Through the glass he watched a rosy-cheeked young woman come towards him. She turned the key, bent to slide back the bolt while Michael waited impatiently.

'Where's my wife?' he demanded as she opened the door.

'I've just woken her with a cup of tea.'

'Daddy!'

Josh came flying down the stairs and flung his arms round his father's waist. Michael could feel the child trembling and was filled with a helpless, protective fury.

'Mrs Dane's been hurt,' Josh said against Michael's jacket,

'and Miss Lucas is really a policewoman. She's been looking after Mummy.'

'Yes, old lad, I know.'

The policewoman gently disengaged Josh. 'Come along, dear, it's time for school and your auntie will be waiting.'

Josh seemed disinclined to let Michael go. 'Will you be here when I get back?' he asked, looking up under the soft fall of hair.

God, what were they doing to him, he and Kate? 'Yes, Josh, I'll be here. I promise.'

He went up the stairs two at a time, swung round at the top of the first flight and started up the second. Kate, wrapping her dressing gown round her, was standing on the landing.

'I heard the bell.'

He had intended to take her straight in his arms, but something in her stance made him hesitate. She added formally, 'Thanks for coming, Michael.'

'I wanted to come last night.' Hell, she might misinterpret that too. He went on quickly, 'Come down and let's talk before that girl gets back. I don't understand how you came to find the body. Was the woman a friend of yours?'

'No, I hardly knew her.' Michael took her arm as they started back to the first floor and felt it shake under his hand. Remembering the Chief Inspector's question, she added more honestly than before, 'I didn't even like her very much. Somehow that makes it worse.'

'Tell me what happened.'

They sat at the kitchen table. Mary Lucas had left coffee on a low light and they drank it slowly while Kate again went through the story. She was just finishing when Richard's voice came from below.

'Kate? May I come up?'

Without waiting for a reply he started up the stairs. Michael's mouth tightened and he rose to his feet, moving round the counter into the living room as the other man reached the top of the stairs.

'Oh!' Richard said flatly, 'You're here.'

'As you see. Can I help you?'

'I came to see how Kate is.' He glanced towards the kitchen but Michael stood his ground.

'She's all right. I'm looking after her.'

'Well, that makes a change!'

'Oh, please!' Kate hurried to join them. 'Don't start arguing. Richard, there's some coffee—'

'I think not,' Michael interrupted. 'Go and get dressed, Kate. Mowbray's just going.'

'I shall go,' Richard said belligerently, 'if and when Kate asks me. She was glad enough of my support last night.'

'I've been hearing about that. Quite a coincidence you were on the doorstep, when you're staying the other side of town.'

Richard's voice rose angrily. 'You can be damn grateful I *was* there. Your wife was in a state of collapse when I found her.'

'Yes, Michael,' Kate put in, peaceably she hoped, 'he was a great help, really. I don't know what I'd have done without him.'

'I see. Then it looks as though I needn't have broken my neck to get here after all.'

Richard snorted. 'Don't give us that. You came for the story, not to hold Kate's hand!'

'Of all the damned—'

'Hey—what is this? World War Three?' Martin had appeared at the top of the stairs. 'You two can be heard all over the building and I'd remind you that, despite everything, we *are* open for business. Lana's off her nut down there in case someone comes in and hears you.'

Michael said shortly, 'I was proposing to take you to sign your statement, Kate, but you're obviously not short of escorts. I promised Josh I'd see him after school so I'll be back at four.'

And without a glance at the other men, he ran down the stairs.

There was a minute's silence, then Richard said quietly, 'I'm sorry, Kate. I shouldn't have let him rile me. Are you up to work today?'

'Yes, I don't want to be alone.'

'Come down when you're ready, then.' He turned to the stairs and Martin, catching Kate's troubled eyes, gave a little shrug and grimace as he followed him. Almost at once, the telephone rang.

'Kate?' It was Madge's shaking voice. 'I've only just heard. I didn't know a thing till that policewoman arrived with Josh. I can't believe it!'

'I know.'

'What time did you get there last night?'

Kate thought back to the glance at her watch in the wet porch. 'Half past nine. Henry asked me to collect that poetry book on the way home.'

'I must have been just ahead of you. I got in as the news was finishing. Kate, I might have passed the murderer!'

'They think she was killed between eight and half past.'

'It's so incredible. Poor, poor Sylvia!'

Kate closed her eyes, remembering the lamplight, the woman in the chair, the obscenely hovering fly.

'You do remember, don't you,' Madge was saying, 'that half term starts today? The school closes at lunchtime.'

'I'd completely forgotten!' Frantically Kate wondered how she could cope with Josh while her own movements were so uncertain. There'd be more visits to the police and she'd have to attend the inquest.

'I'll bring him back here,' Madge said. 'Don't worry about it.'

'Madge'—Kate's grip tightened on the phone—'how—how's Paul?'

'He was a lot better first thing, but this Sylvia business has knocked him for six. We were wondering if there's anything we could do for Henry.'

They talked for a few minutes more, then rang off. Immediately the phone went again.

'Kate?' The crisp, confident voice of her mother-in-law. 'My dear, I've heard the news on the radio and I'm coming straight down to collect you and Josh. I can't imagine what Michael's thinking of, leaving you down there with all those murders going on.'

Kate said weakly, 'But my job—'

'They'll give you a few days off. They must realize you need it. I'll be with you by lunchtime, so have your case packed.'

As she turned from the phone Kate felt a tremendous sense of relief. She didn't know what Michael had told his parents about their problems and at the moment she didn't care. It would be wonderful to have all decisions taken out of her hands, to allow herself to be looked after—most of all, actually to feel safe.

When she reached the shop the atmosphere was fraught. Richard and Martin were monosyllabic, Lana red-eyed and edgy.

Guiltily Kate told them of her mother-in-law's call.

'An excellent idea,' Martin said at once. 'You're in need of a break.'

Kate looked anxiously at Richard and he nodded. 'Don't worry, we can cope. Do you good to get away from Delilah country for a few days.'

Lana sneezed and reached for a handkerchief. 'How's Josh taken the news?'

'He's not been told the full story but he senses something's very wrong. He wanted Michael—Oh God! Michael's coming at four o'clock and we shan't be here. His mother won't have been able to contact him, either.'

'I'll tell him where you are.' Richard smiled grimly. 'Don't worry, I'll be perfectly civil. Now, if you're ready we'd better go down to the station and sign those statements.'

'Right, so what reports have we got in so far?'

Jackson opened the file in front of him. 'The hearth rug was sent to the lab. They'll give us the result as soon as they can. Scenes-of-crime had no joy with wet footprints. Only Mowbray's and Mrs Romilly's showed. What time did the rain start last night, do you remember?'

'I wasn't here. Find out, will you Ken?'

Jackson nodded. 'All hospitals in the area have been checked. No reports of anyone coming in with blood-stained clothing. Mowbray's and Mrs Romilly's fingerprints were taken for elimination, with the expected results. His didn't show, hers came up on the bell and both door handles. Also on the dead woman's hand and in the kitchen. House-to-house inquiries have covered the immediate area and are extending further afield. House and grounds were searched for the weapon, and guess what? No trace. The husband's under sedation but he seems in the clear. There's no doubt he was bedded in at

185

the school from seven o'clock till Flint sought him out to break the news at nine forty-four. Oh, and Collins came up with the dead woman's diary. It was in a locked drawer in her dressing table.'

'Anything of interest?'

'Pretty cryptic. Lots of entries but only initials given. The two latest, both of which appeared at least three times in the last days, were P.N. and R.P. Rumour has it she was having it off with someone from the school, so that's a likely place to start looking.'

'Great. Now we add the entire staff to our list of suspects, and possibly the senior boys too.' He paused. 'You know what's bugging me, Ken?'

'Yep. She's the first victim that hasn't been divorced.'

'Precisely. And that opens up a whole new can of worms. Funny how people clam up, isn't it, when someone dies? I bet they talked their heads off about her while she was alive, but as soon as she's dead they're afflicted with amnesia. Lady Romilly knows more than she's saying, for a start. Might touch on her husband, perhaps, or even the worthy Mowbray. He's the better bet, for my money. I know Mike Romilly and I can't see him taking up with the likes of Sylvia Dane.'

'You reckon Mowbray was the reason they split?'

'We don't know they have. Let's go through Mowbray's movements again and see how the times fit.'

Jackson flicked the papers in front of him. 'In Heatherton till seven-thirty, so was late for his Broadminster appointment, arriving about eight. Old couple in Bridgend Road confirm that in general, but they're not too precise on timing. They did say he stayed for coffee. Mowbray says it was just on nine when he left them. Raining heavily by then and his car wouldn't start.

Leads wet, presumably. Tried to tinker with it for some time. Didn't like to go back to phone because the bedroom light had gone out and he didn't want to disturb the old folk. So eventually he abandons the car and was cutting through Monks' Walk to the taxi rank in Gloucester Street.'

'Um. Doesn't rule him out, does it?'

'Except that he wouldn't be hanging about waiting for the body to be discovered.'

'Unless it was a double bluff. Say he killed her before reaching Bridgend Road "about eight," and then hung around later to be on hand when the body was found. If he'd known Mrs Dane was alone, he also knew her husband was at the school and would be home soon after nine-thirty. He could have done his Samaritan act just as easily with him.'

'Motive?' asked Jackson laconically.

'What motive does this killer ever have, other than a general revenge for deserted husbands? Mowbray fits that category himself. Old Dane was cuckolded all the time and didn't know it. Even Michael Romilly's solo at the moment. Technically all their wives could be at risk. Mrs Dane's bought it. Where's Mowbray's wife, do we know?'

Jackson shrugged. 'Probably safely out of the county.' He paused. 'But Mrs Romilly isn't.' The two men looked at each other. 'You think she might be on the list?'

Webb rubbed a hand over his face. 'She's getting dangerously close.'

The phone sounded and Jackson lifted it. 'OK, Sarge, thanks.' He looked at Webb.

'Speak of the devil. Mowbray and Mrs R are downstairs waiting to sign statements.'

They went down the wide linoleumed steps together. Kate and Richard, sitting uneasily in reception, rose to their feet.

'Car start all right this morning, Mr Mowbray?' Webb asked pleasantly.

Richard met his eyes. 'Yes, thanks. It had dried out by the time I went back for it.'

When the formalities were completed, Kate mentioned her mother-in-law's proposal. 'There wouldn't be any objection, would there, to my being away for a few days?'

'None at all, Mrs Romilly, as long as you can be contacted. How long would it be for?'

'Till Tuesday evening. School starts again on Wednesday.'

'Fine. The inquest's fixed for today week, the fifth of November.' He smiled. 'Don't worry, though, there won't be any fireworks. It's just a question of identification at this stage.'

They walked out to the reception hall and Webb turned to Richard. 'One more question, Mr Mowbray, before you go. Have you sold any knives at all over the last few weeks?'

'Not that I recall. Why?'

'As you know, we haven't found the murder weapon, but it seems custom-built for the purpose. A kitchen knife, for instance, would have bent on contact with muscle. What we're looking for is a shortish, sharp and rigid blade. You've no ideas that could be helpful?'

'Not really. We've a couple of daggers at the shop, but they've not been sold. At least, I don't think so. I'll check when I go back and give you a ring.'

'I'd be most grateful.'

The desk sergeant came across. 'Excuse me, sir, Forensic on the line.'

188

'Thanks, Barton.' He nodded at Richard and Kate, who thankfully took their leave, and went to the desk. Jackson watched him as he nodded a couple of times and made some brief comment down the phone. Old Spiderman was looking tired. Couldn't be much of a life, returning to an empty flat at all hours and having to set to and cook for yourself. Jackson thought briefly of Mrs W., who'd left the Governor for a bloke who worked nine to five and could plan his holidays in advance. Thank heaven for his own cuddly Millie, who always had a cuppa ready no matter what time he got home.

He straightened as Webb put down the phone and came towards him, some of his tiredness dropping away. 'Looks like we've the beginnings of a lead at last. As you know, they took the rug for analysis and they've come up with a few pinpricks of blood. Mixed with traces of soil, they say—reckon it came from a cat's claws. Our furry friend of last night, no doubt. The good news is that the blood group isn't the same as the dead woman's.'

'Not a usefully rare one like AB, by any chance?'

'That's the bad news. Group O, I'm afraid.'

'Well, it narrows the suspects to about twenty thousand.'

'No pine needles this time, but I suppose we can't have everything. So now we embark on checking blood groups, hoping to eliminate a fair number. Get a group of lads organized, will you, Ken. I'll phone Stonebridge with the latest developments. Then I think we've earned ourselves a pie and a pint in the nearest pub. All in the course of duty, mind. You never know what you might learn in a pub!' And with a tired grin, he turned once more to the phone.

CHAPTER 18

Michael arrived at his parents' home on the Saturday evening. Kate, advised of his coming, kept out of the way while he spent some time with Josh. She felt drained, disorientated, knowing this respite was temporary and she'd have to return to the terrors and suspicions of Broadminster.

Her parents-in-law had been gentle and considerate. With surprising forbearance, they'd asked no questions either about the murder or the state of her marriage. Possibly they knew both answers from their son.

When Josh was in bed, Michael came and tapped on her door. 'Hello, Kate. How are you feeling?'

'Exhausted. And frightened.'

He came into the room and closed the door. 'About what? You surely don't think you're in danger?' She shrugged, too weary to explain, but he persisted. 'Tell me.'

Kate sat on the bed staring at clasped hands. After a moment, as Michael stood waiting, she said unwillingly, 'It's getting more and more personal, this Delilah business. Remember how you said at the beginning I was taking more interest in it than usual? Even then, though I couldn't define it, I felt threatened.'

'Threatened?' Michael's voice sharpened. 'Why should you?'

She shrugged again, shoulders moving under the silk of her blouse. 'For one thing, I've had some kind of link with three of the victims. You knew the first one, Martin the third, all of us the fifth. It seems to be—closing in.'

'How well did Martin know the third victim?'

'He'd been to see her on business the week she was killed. In fact he'd gone back on the actual day, but changed his mind.'

'Or so he says.'

'I think I believe him. And, oh Michael, I'm so worried about Paul!'

He stared at her. 'Why on earth?'

'Because I—I think he was having an affair with Sylvia. The police are bound to find out, and perhaps Madge will.'

'*Paul*? Having an affair? I don't believe it.'

'He called round twice when she was alone.'

Under Michael's questioning, Kate related the occasions and Paul's behaviour on the night of the dinner party.

'You didn't tell the police?'

'How could I? I don't think he *killed* her, for heaven's sake.' She looked up quickly. 'You won't say anything, will you? To Chief Inspector Webb?'

Michael looked at her strangely. 'I know you've a poor opinion of me, Kate, but I don't shop my friends.'

She bit her lip and he stared down at her, the drooping dark head above the creamy silk of her blouse.

'We'd better go down,' he said brusquely. 'I came to tell you there's sherry waiting.' Mrs Romilly was a slim and elegant sixty, well dressed, well coiffured, well content with her role in life.

She liked things to run on predictable lines in an orderly fashion and did her best to make them conform. She played bridge and golf, delivered meals on wheels, and was on the committee of the Women's Conservative Club. She would have preferred her son to go into law like her barrister husband, but she was proud enough of his achievements, fond of her daughter-in-law, and devoted to her grandson. Exactly what this nonsense was about Michael and Kate living apart she was not sure, but it was time they pulled themselves together, for their own sakes as well as Josh's. All three of them looked pale and unhappy.

The talk during dinner was superficial, a rule of the house. Mrs Romilly believed weighty topics overshadowed her cuisine and led to indigestion. But round the drawing room fire with coffee, as Kate well knew, the subjects close to her heart and her curiosity were sure to be raised.

'You're not looking well, Kate,' she began purposefully, refilling her cup. 'It's really most unfortunate that you're in the thick of these murders.'

'They're pretty spread out, Mother,' Michael said politically. 'The first was in Shillingham, remember.'

'I'm surprised, dear, that your policeman friend hasn't found the killer before this. I thought he was a good man.'

'He is, but he's only human. They're turning the country upside down, but if they've come up with anything concrete, they're playing it close to their chests.'

'It took five years to catch the Yorkshire Ripper,' Bruce Romilly commented.

'Those murders were at longer intervals,' his wife pointed out. 'There have been five in Broadshire in only two months, the last three in *three weeks*, for heaven's sake!'

'Nevertheless,' Michael said stoutly, 'I've a high opinion of Webb. He's a complex character and not easy to get to know, but he's first-class at his job.'

'How complex?'

'For a start he's a brilliant cartoonist. He could have made a career of it, but he regards it as a hobby.'

'A satirical policeman?' Mrs Romilly said lightly. 'Well, well!'

'You need the same approach for both jobs, a discerning eye and the knack of probing beneath the surface. What's more surprising is that he also has a flair for watercolours.'

'Does he sell them commercially?' Mr Romilly asked.

'The paintings? He's never tried. I have to twist his arm to get the cartoons.'

'You publish them, Michael?'

'All I can lay my hands on. There'll be nothing for months, but when I badger him a bulky envelope arrives with a dozen or more.'

'I must look out for them. How does he sign himself?'

'An S in a circle, meaning a spider in a "Webb".' Michael finished his coffee. 'He told me once he used them to solve his cases.'

'A form of relaxation, I suppose, to clear the mind.'

'I think it's more that the caricatures are so recognizable they could pinpoint a trait he'd only noticed subconsciously.'

'It doesn't sound very scientific,' Mrs Romilly objected.

'Nor are hunches, but they're often right. Of course that's only the starting point, but the initial spark can come from anywhere.'

Kate leaned back and closed her eyes. The firelight was warm on her face, flickering redly against her closed lids. If only it were over, she thought tiredly, not just the murders but their own personal problems. What was Jill doing while Michael was away? She felt the nearness of tears and bent to put down her cup.

'Would you mind if I go to bed? I'm very tired.'

She had started up the stairs when the drawing-room door opened and closed again and she turned to see Michael looking up at her.

'I presume you're not expecting me to join you?' She stared at him numbly and after a moment he went on, 'Don't worry, I'll sleep in my old room.'

Without a word she turned and went on up the stairs.

The pathologist's report had been waiting for Webb when he returned to Headquarters on the Friday evening. It contained no surprises. He glanced through it, extracting the points that interested him. Thorax entered traumatically by instrument 1.8 centimetres wide through third and fourth intercostal space... Downward tract of incision consistent with thrust from assailant standing opposite seated victim. Death timed at shortly after 20.00, which, Webb reflected, made verification of Mowbray's movements of paramount importance.

Contents of the stomach revealed partially digested meal of curried beef and rice eaten some two hours before death. No mystery about that; the leftovers were in the fridge in Monks' Walk. For the rest, there was an appendix scar but no other distinguishing marks. And no defence wounds, indicating that Sylvia Dane, like her predecessors, had been taken by surprise.

Webb put the report on one side and pulled towards him a sheaf of statements resulting from the ever-widening inquiries. The top ones related to the Larksworth case and his interest quickened as he saw the word 'moped' underlined. A stallholder remembered seeing one in the vicinity—and there'd been a similar report after the Shillingham murder.

Webb made reference to this at the briefing half an hour later and detailed Standing and Ridley to check known owners of such vehicles. Afterwards, when the others had dispersed, Fleming approached him.

'I'd like to see some of these people myself now, Dave, put faces to names. I suggest we go and root them out on Sunday—they should be home then and you prefer to see them on their own ground, don't you?'

'I do, sir, but if you'd rather—'

'No, no, I'm happy to go along with that. Be glad to get out of this damned room. And people are less careful what they say at home. We'll start with the staff at the shop. They're always cropping up, what with Bailey's visit to Otterford and the others finding the body. And have we checked on antique knockers? The hint of a fortune in the attic will overcome any woman's caution.'

'We put out feelers, yes sir, but there's no report of knockers in the area lately.'

'Bear it in mind, anyway. Now, where do all these people live? Spread round the bloody county, I suppose.'

'Pretty well, yes. Bailey down in Broadminster, and Mrs Romilly, though she's away for a few days. Miss Truscott, if you're including her, is at Littlemarsh, and Mowbray's up in Chipping Claydon.'

'Ye gods! We'd better make an early start, then.'

Since he was not to be his own agent over the weekend, Webb had a quick word with Jackson. 'I've told Standing and Ridley to get onto you if they've any luck with mopeds. In the meantime, go through Mowbray's statement with a fine-tooth comb. His movements and the time of Mrs Dane's death are crucial. Oh, and Ken'—Jackson, on his way to the door, turned back—'I want a note of every bloody pine tree in the country!'

In fact, nothing spectacular emerged over the weekend. Bailey and his girlfriend had gone to London for two days, so that interview, like Kate Romilly's, had to be postponed. Nor was the one with Lana Truscott too successful. She was unwilling even to let them in the house.

'I seem to have caught another cold,' she told them nasally. 'I don't want to pass it on, and there's nothing I can tell you anyway.'

'Don't worry about the cold, Miss Truscott.' Fleming said firmly, and stood his ground until, sneezing protestingly, she admitted them. Sitting on the chintzy sofa, they put their questions to her one by one. No, she'd not seen strangers in the neigh-bourhood. Yes, she was sure no weapons had been sold lately. Her only spark of animation came when Fleming said smoothly, 'You know, of course, that Mrs Romilly met Mr Mowbray when she ran for help. Were you aware that he was in the neighbourhood that evening?'

Surprisingly, her face flamed and she rubbed agitatedly at her arm. 'Mr Mowbray works irregular hours,' she said stiffly. 'I keep a note of some of his appointments, but often one leads directly to another.'

'But did you know where he was that evening?'

'No.'

'All of you at the shop knew Mrs Dane, I believe?' Webb tactfully veered off at a tangent.

'Slightly, yes. She was one of our main exhibitors.'

'Had you ever met her socially?'

196

'Never.' Lana set her lips tightly.

'Not even at the private view?'

'I wasn't at the view, Chief Inspector, but if I had been, it would have been a business engagement, not a social one.'

'I see. Of course.'

'So if there's nothing else I can tell you—'

She rose to her feet and the two men perforce rose with her.

'One final request,' Webb said unexpectedly. 'Would it be possible to see your father?'

'My father?' She stared at him blankly.

'Just a courtesy call, as I'm in the house.'

'He's probably asleep. I don't think—'

'We wouldn't stay long.' He'd been impressed by the old man during their association over the son's death and didn't want to leave without passing the time of day. Smiling pleasantly, he waited until Lana Truscott reluctantly showed them upstairs. The two policemen stood looking out of the window while the invalid was propped up and his pillows arranged.

'He's ready now,' Lana said shortly. 'I'll go and make some tea.'

Webb turned and smiled at the old man. He had gone down-hill in the six months since he'd seen him. The flesh of his face had fallen away so that nose and eyebrows jutted forward, giving him, with his feathery white hair, the appearance of an old eagle.

'I hope you'll forgive us disturbing you, Mr Truscott.'

'Delighted to see you, Chief Inspector. I don't have many visitors. I suppose you're here about the unpleasant business in Broadminster. Lana will help you all she can, but for myself I only know what she tells me. I'm ashamed to say, I spend most of my time asleep these days.'

'The days must drag when your daughter's at work,' Fleming

said sympathetically. 'You should have a pet to keep you company.'

The old man sighed. 'Lana says dogs are messy creatures and she's enough to do without cleaning up after them. And she's allergic to cats, so they're out too. I might just be allowed a budgie, provided,' he added with a mischievous smile, 'it didn't spill its seed!' He shook his head in gentle reproof. 'I shouldn't speak like that. Lana's the most devoted daughter. She does all she can to make my life bearable.'

Lana herself came in at that point with the tea tray, and the Chief Superintendent gallantly stood to help her. Webb watched him sardonically, seeing the woman's pale face soften into a slight smile. A way with the ladies, had old Fleming, smooth and polished, but it had produced no results here. In fact, Webb thought resignedly, the only new fact to emerge from their visit was her reaction to Richard Mowbray's name, and that was hardly relevant to their inquiries.

Later, at Chipping Claydon, Webb wondered what women saw in Mowbray. He wasn't good-looking by conventional standards and his pallor struck the countryman in Webb as distinctly unhealthy. Added to which something about his eyes, flat and watchful like a snake's, made the hair rise on the Chief Inspector's neck. Still, you couldn't work on the assumption that everyone you disliked was a murderer.

'Interesting collection of weapons you have here, sir,' he said blandly, nodding to a display on the left of the fireplace.

'One of my hobbies. Those are sixteenth-century rapiers, with companion daggers. An interesting fact is that the daggers are left-handed.' He met Webb's eyes coolly, and the Chief Inspector felt he was being dared to comment further.

'Fascinating, fascinating,' Fleming murmured, seating himself in a wing chair and feeling for his pipe. 'Have you any objection if I smoke?'

Mowbray turned to him, his momentary tension easing, and Webb seated himself on the sofa. He was aware that his dislike was mutual and felt it would be politic to leave the talking to his superior. Meanwhile he looked about him with grudging approval. Lovely house it was, perched above the village like an eyrie. And that was presumably the ex-wife looking broodingly down on them. An excellent painting, but Webb was glad he'd no likeness of Susan on his own walls. Even her snapshots had been thrown out when she left, not from any sense of drama but because they were no longer relevant.

From his wife, he thought briefly of Hannah, aware of the need building up to see her again. Though Mowbray couldn't know it, he was in a similar position to Webb himself. Was he hoping Mrs Romilly would be his Hannah? Webb couldn't see it happening. The girl was a different mould, softer, more dependent. A 'no strings' arrangement would leave her hopelessly adrift—Mowbray was a fool if he couldn't see it.

Michael left his parents' home on the Sunday evening and as he went up his own path he heard the telephone ringing. Swearing under his breath, he hurried to get the key in and the door open before it stopped.

'Hello? Romilly speaking.'

'Hi, Michael. Dave Webb here.'

'Oh, hello.' Michael pushed the door shut with his foot. 'What can I do for you?'

'I'd be glad of a little press help, if you could arrange it.'

'Sure. Spell it out.'

'I reckon the killer must be pretty pleased with himself, watching the police running round in circles. Probably fancies himself no end. We might be able to use that against him.'

'How?'

'By pretending we think it's someone else. A murderer's ego is often his Achilles heel.'

'So what can we do?'

'I'd like you to run a story along the lines that the police are closing in. Throw in, without specific quotes, that we're anxious to trace a red-haired man of about forty-two, height six foot, broad build, with a Bristol accent.'

Michael, jotting down the particulars, grinned in the darkness. 'Does that mean all tall, red-haired Bristolians are in the clear?'

He heard Webb laugh. 'Pretty well. The description's off the top of my head. It's worth a try—let's see what it brings forth. Sorry to phone so late, by the way. I tried earlier but there was no reply.'

'I've been at my parents' for the weekend.'

'Ah. See your wife there?'

'It must be bloody marvellous to be a detective.'

'OK, OK, I only asked! Night then, Michael.'

'Good night.'

Michael stood for a moment frowning down at the phone. Then, with a gesture of dismissal, he snapped on the lights and set about preparing for bed.

At the other side of town Webb was conscious of having missed something, something which he knew instinctively was important. For a while he tried to flail his tired mind into recalling it. Then, climbing into bed, he abandoned it. Perhaps it would come back to him in the morning.

The following Tuesday Mrs Romilly drove Kate and Josh back to Monks' Walk—'Against my will,' she told Kate as, after a cup of tea, she went on her way. 'I'd be much happier if you stayed with us till everything's cleared up.'

There was a note from Madge in the letter box. 'Subdued celebrations this year, but could you and Josh come to supper on the third?'

That was tomorrow—Madge's birthday. Kate hoped Paul had come to terms with Sylvia's death and not aroused his wife's suspicions.

'Enjoy your break?' Martin greeted her on her appearance in the shop. 'We've been grilled by the fuzz in your absence! No doubt your turn will come.'

'I've had more than my share already.'

Later, over coffee, Lana said, 'I didn't think you'd come back.'

'It was only a half-term visit—I told you.'

'Wasn't your husband there?'

'Briefly.'

'I hoped once you were away from here, you'd come together.'

'I'm afraid things have gone too far for that.'

The words stayed ominously in Kate's mind for the rest of the day.

When she reached the Netherbys' house, Madge greeted her warmly. 'It's ages since we've seen you, Kate. How are you?'

'All right, thanks. Happy birthday.' She proffered her parcel and Madge unwrapped it as excitedly as a child. It was a porcelain vase from the shelves of Pennyfarthings.

'How lovely, Kate! Thank you so much, the colour's perfect. Come and see what Paul's given me.'

She flung open the dining-room door and stood to one side. Propped against the far wall was a large portrait of the Netherby children. They were laughing, their heads together, as lifelike as a mirror image. Except that the artist revealed more than a mirror, an indefinable essence of the children themselves. Kate stood immobile, aware of implications she had not yet grasped. Behind her, Madge said softly, 'You know who painted it, don't you?'

Yes, suddenly she knew. The artist could only be Sylvia Dane. It was a moment of truth and Kate wasn't equal to it. Shame, relief, and understanding fused in her head, and to Madge's consternation she burst into tears. Immediately Madge's arm went round her.

'Oh love, I'm sorry. Did it bring it all back? Come and have a drink. You'll feel better in a moment.'

She led Kate to the kitchen where Paul, expressing concern, poured her a small brandy.

'I didn't know a thing about it,' Madge was saying. 'Paul supplied her with photos and she managed with only a couple of sittings.' Kate recalled Sylvia explaining that very method.

'We nearly let it slip a couple of times,' Paul put in. 'Like Sylvia knowing I'd been in Otterford the day of the murder. But my trusting little wife, bless her, merely assumed Henry'd told her.' He laid his hand over Madge's and smiled at her and Kate burned with shame for her own doubts of him.

'Poor Sylvia,' Paul continued. 'Not knowing her love life was common knowledge, she thought I went to ridiculous lengths to conceal my visits. They could have been misconstrued, though.

I collected the painting during a free period and sneaked it home when Madge was at the dentist. We never guessed it was the last thing she'd do.'

'It's beautiful, Paul,' Kate said unsteadily. 'A lovely thought and a lovely present.' And to their surprise, she leaned over and kissed his cheek.

By the time the children came through, Kate had regained her composure and with it a little of her faith in human nature. She must let Michael know her doubts of Paul were unfounded.

Intercepting her thought, Madge asked quietly, 'Was Michael at his mother's?'

'Just for the weekend.'

'And?'

Kate shook her head. Madge's marriage was secure after all, but there'd been no improvement in her own.

Later that evening, as Kate was thinking of bed, the doorbell suddenly rang through the flat, shattering the peaceful calm. At once her heart set up its familiar, muffled beating and all the fears she'd tried to bury reared up to face her again. She eased herself out of her chair and stood listening, jumping as the impatient clarion sounded again. Swiftly she moved to the window, lifting the curtain aside, but the street was deserted and the broad sill hid anyone standing directly below.

Despairingly, Kate knew she must go down. It was worse to stand here wondering than to face what was below. Slowly she started down the stairs, pausing at the bend to peer ahead to the rectangle of glass in the front door. No one was outlined against it. Not the Chief Inspector, then, as she'd half-expected. Perhaps some passing youths had simply pressed her bell. Twice?

Eyes unwaveringly on the glass pane, Kate moved down the

narrow hallway. A car whooshed past outside and its lights briefly raked the door. She had reached it now and stood motionless, every nerve geared to sounds from outside. There were none. Inch by inch she slid back the bolt and turned the key, guiding it with her fingers so that it did not clatter back. She had her hands on the knob and she started to turn it when laughing voices sounded in the distance. If people were about, she should be safe. In one swift movement she pulled the door open and then gasped as something soft and heavy which had been propped against it fell inwards onto her feet.

It was several long seconds before, in the uncertain light, Kate dared to bend down and look more closely. Heaped grotesquely in front of her lay a dead pigeon, the soft bloom of its feathers stained with blood. A label was tied round its neck and Kate knew its message with numb certainty. 'For Delilah.'

Her frozen paralysis splintered; she tried with both hands to push the door shut but the soft unwieldy bundle was in the way. Sobbing, gasping, she continued to strain ineffectually against it until in desperation she steeled herself to push out the obstruction with her shoe. The bolt was beyond her rubbery fingers, but she turned the key before, shaking and stumbling, she fled back up the stairs to the telephone. No time for the directory. With maddening slowness the dial completed its full turn three times. 'Police!' she heard herself say. 'Chief Inspector Webb. I must see him *now*!'

CHAPTER 19

Oh God, I never thought it would come to this. I wish I could stop, but I can't. No one else will do it, and the purge must go on.

The police think they're clever, but they're on the wrong track. Suppose I went to Webb and said, 'You fool! I did it!'? It would be worth it, to see his expression.

I'm very aware of expressions now. Sylvia Dane's, for instance, so superior and condescending, though she'd the morals of an alley cat. And Mrs Forbes, as fresh and wholesome as her new bread, yet according to the paper she'd had three lovers in as many months.

I thought Kate Romilly was different, but I was wrong. She's the same as the others and I can't make exceptions. The sentence must be carried out.

CHAPTER 20

Webb said carefully, 'I'm not trying to frighten you, Mrs Romilly. Every psycho in the country has fantasies about Delilah and this may not have any link with the murders. On the other hand, it could be the lead we've been waiting for. It's a pity you didn't report the earlier incidents.'

Kate's eyes were large and frightened. 'I was so sure it was those boys who'd pestered me.'

'It still might be, but better safe than sorry. Can you think of anyone else who might try to frighten you?'

She shook her head. 'It's so pointless.'

'Well, I'm going to get Miss Lucas over here. Till this is cleared up, she'll be in the flat with you all the time. I'll also arrange for an officer to keep watch outside and follow you at a distance when you leave the premises. What's the matter?'

Kate was staring at him, her hands to her face. 'I've just remembered, there *was* a man watching me. Or at least, he might have been. He was there several times, on a bench on the Green.'

'When was that?'

'About a month ago, I suppose.'

'And you haven't seen him since?'

'No. At first I used to look all the time, then I forgot about it.'

'What kind of man was he?' Wryly, Webb thought of the mythical redhead from Bristol.

'I didn't see him properly. He had thick dark hair and wore jeans. That's all I can tell you. Lana said he was in his thirties.'

'Miss Truscott saw him too?'

'Yes, it was she who pointed him out. She'd seen him several times.'

'And how often did you see him?'

'Only the once, actually. Perhaps he realized we'd spotted him.'

'Was this before or after you received the first package?'

'Soon after, because when I saw him I immediately thought of the moth.'

'Nobody who looked similar came into the shop or contacted you out in the street?' 'No, no one.'

'Right. From now on you'll have police protection, but you must tell no one about it. *No one*, you understand?' Kate nodded. 'Can you impress that on your little boy without frightening him?'

'I'll try.'

Webb looked at her consideringly. At least she was now frightened herself, as he'd intended. He was appalled at the chances she'd been taking. Even the significance of the death's-head moth had escaped her. She'd interpreted as youthful malice what might have been a serious death threat. There was no way of knowing if the gruesome offering had indeed come from 'Delilah'. If so, it was a new departure to the best of Webb's knowledge. But at best it was a nasty case of victimization and he couldn't afford to ignore it.

He said more gently, 'Miss Lucas will be as unobtrusive as possible.' And as Kate still looked apprehensive, added less than truthfully, 'It shouldn't be for long. We're closing in on him now.'

'Yes, I saw that in the paper.'

Webb's face was expressionless. 'There's the inquest on Friday, don't forget. Would you like us to send a car for you?'

'No, thank you, I expect I'll be going with Richard—Mr Mowbray.'

With admitted prejudice, Webb wondered darkly if Richard Mowbray ran a line in dead pigeons.

It was eleven-thirty when, having handed over to Mary Lucas, he left Monks' Walk and there was still the protection to arrange before he could sign off. He carried the pigeon gingerly into Court Lane police station and dropped it in front of the desk sergeant, who backed away with exaggerated alarm.

'This could be an exhibit, Barton. Have it gone over, will you, then put it in deep freeze somewhere.'

'I'd rather put it in a pie, myself!'

'And let Henderson get to work on the label. Who's in the building?'

Barton consulted his list. 'Flint, Ridley, Standing, Harrison—'

'Harrison'll do. Get him here at the double, I've an urgent job waiting.'

Twelve hours later, Sergeant Jackson sat down opposite Webb in the Incident Room at Headquarters. 'We've traced the initials in the diary. You were right—they were both at the school. Standing went along there yesterday. First chance we had, with the place being shut for half term. Came up with two P.N.'s and no less than three R.P.'s on the staff list but we weeded them down to Paul Netherby and Robin Peters.'

'Either of them likely to be Chummie?'

'Very doubtful, I'd say. Paul Netherby'd commissioned a painting of his kids for his wife's birthday.'

'Could have been a cover-up.'

'Don't think so. Seemed a straight sort of bloke. He kept popping in to see how it was going, that's all. The other one, though, Robin Peters, he was something different. Started blustering before we even opened our mouths.'

Webb leaned back in his chair, the tips of his fingers together. 'What's he like?'

'Thirties. Not bad-looking. Academic type.'

'Thirties? Cradle-snatching, was she?'

'Seems she liked them young. Our Mr Peters wasn't too gallant—insisted he wasn't the only member of staff involved with her.'

'Married, I suppose?'

'Oh yes. Couple of young kids.'

'Wife know anything about it?'

'Not so far. That's what was bugging him.'

'So once more we've come up with sweet F.A.'

'Looks like it. I'm willing to bet Peters hasn't the stomach for murder, but in any case he had the same alibi as Dane—at the school all evening seeing parents.'

The phone rang and Webb reached for it. He listened intently for a minute, muttered an expletive, and then, with a few quick words, dropped the phone and started to his feet.

'Come on, Ken, we're on the road again. Otterford this

time. Seems some woman did see the moped there—hadn't thought it was important, for God's sake. What's more, she got a look at the rider.'

'Didn't take a note of his number, I suppose?'

'You want jam on it!'

It was a foggy day, damp and smelling of sulphur but despite the weather Otterford market was in full swing. With collars up and caps over their ears, the stallholders stoically plied their wares and the villagers just as stoically bought them. Moisture dripped off the awnings and collected in puddles on the uneven pavements. Behind the village square an assortment of vans and trucks merged into the thick air.

'No sign of a ruddy moped today!' Jackson said disgustedly. They'd had to park some distance from the police station and were walking in single file along the narrow pavement, jolted by prams and shopping trolleys. A smell of fish and chips assaulted them from an open doorway and a wet, miserable-looking queue straggled onto the street, patiently awaiting their turn. Jackson's stomach growled in sympathy. It seemed a long time since breakfast.

The last in a row of council houses doubled as a police station, a blue globe over its front door. A single-storey extension had been built onto one side and it was from this that the village constable, seeing their arrival, emerged to meet them.

'PC Simpson, sir. We have met. My wife was wondering if you'd like a cuppa before we start?'

'That would be very welcome. Thank you.'

'She could make a round of sandwiches, and all,' the constable added eagerly. 'You've not had your dinner, I suppose?'

Webb hesitated, caught the gleam in Jackson's eye. 'If you're sure it's no trouble.'

They followed Simpson round the side of the house and he ushered them into a small square room. It contained a desk and telephone, two chairs, and a filing cabinet. There was room for little else. On the wall hung an official notice board and an ordnance survey map. Constable Simpson showed them to the seats and disappeared briefly through an internal door, reappearing with a spindly dining chair.

'The food won't be long,' he assured them. 'June's seeing to it now.' He was a red-faced young man with a figure that would once have been described as portly. Cautiously he lowered himself onto the narrow chair, placing his hands squarely on his spreading thighs.

'It was market day that brought it back, like,' he said conversationally, and seeing their blank faces, added in explanation, 'Mrs Parker, that is. Seeing the moped. I passed her on my beat and she stopped to chat. Quite a chatterbox is Mrs Parker. And that ties in, too. She said, "All the pleasure's gone out of market days now, Constable. I keep thinking of that poor Mrs Percival." And I said, "It could jog your memory, though. Remind you of a face, or a car, or that moped we're trying to trace."'

A tap on the door heralded Mrs Simpson bearing a tray filled with mugs of steaming tea and a plate piled high with sandwiches. The bread was fresh and the butter, thickly spread, formed a layer of its own over which succulent slices of pink ham had been laid. This was what Jackson called a sandwich. As they started to eat, Constable Simpson, munching steadily, went on with his recital as though there'd been no interruption.

'"Moped?" she said. "Lord love us, I saw one of them. On

the day it happened, too. Went clean out of my head till you mentioned it." Seems she'd collected the kids from school—three-thirty it must have been, or just after, because she'd only got to the corner of Pond Lane. That's the next turning after Westfield Close, where the murder took place.'

Webb, taking a sip of the scalding tea, wondered if it would be necessary to see the woman at all after this verbatim preview.

'Well, she'd stopped to talk to a friend—Mrs Parker all over. I've watched her progress through the village and she never gets more than a few yards before she stops to talk to someone. Fair chatterbox, like I said.'

Takes one to know one, Webb thought humorously.

'And while she was talking, the little 'un had wandered to the edge of the pavement and was scuffing at the leaves in the gutter. Suddenly there was a screech of tyres and this moped comes roaring round the corner of Westfield Close. He saw the kid in the gutter and swerved, like. Almost came off. Then away he roared down the street and out of sight.'

Simpson wiped the back of his hand across his mouth and looked at his audience with satisfaction. 'So I says to her, "You'd best have a word with the Chief Inspector, you had."'

Mrs Parker proved to be a thin young woman with pale, prominent eyes and a head of frizzy hair standing up like a halo. She ushered them into her front room with nervous ceremony, her face pink with importance. A large black cat was asleep on the most comfortable seat and Webb paused, expecting Mrs Parker to remove it. When she did not, he pointedly seated himself on an upright chair against the wall.

'Right, Mrs Parker. Constable Simpson here thinks you might have some information for us.'

As he'd suspected, the constable had spiked her guns. Her story followed an identical pattern to his, in almost the same words they had been regaled with over lunch.

'I was that frightened, Inspector,' she finished.

'Chief Inspector,' interpolated Simpson reprovingly.

'Oh, sorry I'm sure. Such a mouthful though, isn't it? Anyway, I had visions of little Lee under those wheels. I screamed—I did really—and rushed to pick him up. And that's how I saw the chap's face—we were only inches apart.'

'And can you describe him, Mrs Parker?' Here, after all, was the nub of the matter.

'Well, he looked frightened. Probably because I screamed, though of course he was wearing a helmet so I don't know how much he heard. And his eyes were large and staring.'

'Did you get an impression of his height and build?'

'Can't say I did, really. Not height, because he didn't actually come off his bike. But he wasn't very broad. Narrow shoulders and that. I got the feeling he was only a lad, though I'm not sure why.'

'So that's it,' Webb commented on the way back to Headquarters. 'Of course it's possible it wasn't the same moped in all three places—there are plenty about—but unlikely, I'd say. The fact that one was seen near three of the crimes must be significant. But why didn't it figure in the Broadminster ones? Or was it just that no one there noticed it?'

'He might live there, and not need the bike.'

'Possibly. But Mrs Dane's the odd one out in other ways too. The only victim who wasn't divorced, and the only one killed in

213

the evening. There may be something in both those facts. Her name hadn't appeared in the papers, after all, and though her goings-on were well known in Broadminster, *it was only among people who knew her*. It looks as though at this late stage of the game we come back to our original theory, that she actually knew her killer. Or at least he knew her.'

'And the evening call?'

'It could have been a lover, though not Robin Peters, if he was tied up at the school.' 'You're sure he couldn't have slipped out briefly? That end of Monks' Walk is only round the corner from St Benedict's.'

'No chance whatsoever. He had appointments at ten-minute intervals all evening.'

Webb sucked his teeth reflectively. 'We're overlooking something, Ken. Something that's staring us in the face. We've enough facts now to nail him, if we can just fit them together.'

Jackson grinned. 'Time to go walkabout, Guy?'

'I think it is. There's the inquest tomorrow but I'll take Saturday off and see if I can come up with something. Let's hope for a fine day.'

Mary Lucas's presence at breakfast took Josh by surprise, which, after she received a message on her radio, gave way to a sense of importance. He bet none of the other boys had the police staying with them and sending messages and things.

'We don't want anyone to know, though, Josh,' Mary told him earnestly. 'Do you think you can keep it a secret?'

'Of course I can.' He hesitated, then added frankly, 'Though I'd *like* everyone to know.'

'Tell you what, then. If you keep quiet, we'll let you tell

them later, and I'll arrange for you to have a ride in a police car. Would you like that?'

'It'd be great! Could Tim come too?'

'I should think so, but only if you don't say a word till we tell you.'

'Isn't Mummy going to tell anyone either?'

'Not a soul.'

'Not even Daddy?'

Mary hesitated, but Kate said steadily, 'Not even Daddy for the moment, but we will later.'

Josh considered this. 'OK,' he said then, and reached for the cornflakes. Over his head, Kate and Mary exchanged a look of relief.

It was half-day closing again—how quickly Thursdays came round—and Kate wondered apprehensively if she'd feel restricted with the policewoman constantly on hand.

But Mary Lucas said cheerfully, 'Just carry on as usual. What do you normally do on Thursday afternoons?'

Kate pulled a face. 'Have a cleaning blitz, if I'm at home.'

'I'll give you a hand if you like.'

So while Mary set about dusting the living room, Kate humped the vacuum cleaner upstairs and pushed open Josh's door. The sun was shining through the skylight and the small room was warm and cheerful. Methodically she started to fold the jerseys which were thrown over the chair and put them neatly in a drawer. Her son had certainly stamped his character on the room, Kate thought with amusement. A large poster of a racing car was fastened with blue tack above his bed and on the notice board he'd pinned a selection of drawings. One had slipped to the floor, and Kate bent to retrieve it. The side uppermost was a printed form headed Broadcasting Research Listening Panel, with a list of questions below. Where had Josh found that? She flipped it over and recognized the drawing of an improbably long-legged calf which he'd brought back from his day at the Truscotts'. She pinned it back on the board, biting her lip as she saw the illustration alongside, labelled, in case of doubt, 'Auntie Jill making a cake'. She wished passionately that she was herself baking a cake in her kitchen at Shillingham, not cooped up here under police protection.

Her wave of misery was interrupted by Mary's cheerful voice from below, and, brushing self-pity aside, Kate went down to join her.

Kate had been dreading the inquest, but in fact it lasted only minutes, then was adjourned for a month while the police completed their investigations. She and Richard gave evidence of finding the body and the pathologist stated the cause of death. Chief Inspector Webb was on hand as well as a neat, grey-haired man she hadn't seen before, who seemed to be his superior. Webb introduced him afterwards as Chief Superintendent Fleming and they exchanged a few words.

'He and Webb came to see me last Sunday,' Richard told her as they went down the steps of the court. 'A much more congenial man than the Chief Inspector. Doesn't treat you as though you ought to be behind bars.'

'You think Webb does?'

'Very definitely.'

'I rather like him. He can look forbidding, but when he smiles he's quite different.'

'He's never smiled at me,' Richard said. 'Come on, we'll treat ourselves to lunch before we go back.'

Kate was surprised when Richard drew up not outside one of the pubs but in the forecourt of the Consort Hotel. Seeing the small Ford follow them in, she hoped with a touch of amusement that her shadow could claim expenses.

For the Consort was one of Broadminster's newest and most luxurious hotels. The cocktail lounge was all glass and chrome, with olive-green seating and enormous plants. It was rather, Kate thought, like being in a fish tank. But the seats were comfortable and she leant back and allowed her eyes to close. The clink of a glass on the table brought them open again. Richard sat down opposite her and raised his own.

'Confusion to our enemies!'

'Have we any?' Kate smiled.

'Certainly. Everyone has.'

'What a philosophy!' But she was thinking of the dead pigeon and the things that had gone before. Chillingly, Richard was right; she herself certainly had enemies. Possibly he included the Chief Inspector among his. During all the years that Michael had spoken of Webb, Kate never imagined she would meet him, least of all in connection with a murder case. But she'd liked him, and was surprised by Richard's antipathy. *Did* the Chief Inspector think he should be 'behind bars'? The possibility of Richard's being on his list of suspects revived her own doubts about him. What had he been doing at Sylvia's gate? He'd offered no explanation and she hadn't liked to ask.

Lunchtime drinkers now crowded the bar, calling to each other, laughing, enjoying an amicable if fleeting camaraderie. After a while Richard ordered smoked salmon sandwiches. They were cold—out of a fridge?—and the bread felt slightly damp. Kate wasn't hungry but she ate two of the triangles and Richard finished them. She was aware of a feeling of claustrophobia. Loud voices hemmed them in on all sides, the heat from the pipes behind her made her head ache, and the massed vegetation seemed vaguely threatening. She was glad when it was time to go. After the green stretches of the cocktail lounge, Pennyfarthings seemed small and safe and familiar.

Kate was alone in the shop when Michael arrived the next morning. His eyes as they met hers were hard and cold.

'Enjoy your lunch yesterday?' And, as she stared at him, he added, 'I was driving past as you came out.'

'I didn't see you.'

'Obviously. You were too interested in your companion.'

Kate drew a steadying breath. 'We'd been to the inquest. I thought you might have been there.'

'I can't be everywhere, Kate. John Darby was covering it.'

'But you knew I'd have to attend.'

'So?'

She raised her head. 'I thought you might come to offer moral support.'

'Three's a crowd. I knew Mowbray'd be holding your hand.'

'As Jill holds yours.'

His mouth tightened. 'We're quits, then.'

'Does she—has she moved in with you?'

'What's it to you?'

'Has she, Michael?'

'It's none of your business. I don't inquire how often your boyfriend creeps upstairs to visit you.'

Kate gasped, her resentment fuelled by the fact that she'd refused Richard out of loyalty to Michael. 'You're vile!' she choked her voice rising. 'If that's your opinion of me, you can go to hell. I never want to see you again!'

His eyes slid past her and she spun round. Framed in the office doorway were Lana, Richard, and Josh, all pale-faced and staring at them. How much had they heard?

Josh said in a high, quavering little voice, 'Daddy?' And as Kate made a convulsive movement towards him, Michael, face blazing, bent down and held out his arms. The child rushed into them. Michael scooped him up, turned on his heel, and strode out of the shop. The door rocked to behind him. Kate stood unmoving, her hands over her face, feeling the tears drip through her fingers. Richard's arms came round her, pulling her gently towards him.

'All right, it's over now. He's gone.'

If the words were meant to soothe her, they had the opposite effect. Leaning helplessly against him, Kate abandoned herself to a storm of weeping.

CHAPTER 21

Webb was not able, as he'd intended, to take the day off that Saturday. Fleming had called a special briefing and, arising from it, a stack of extra work needed his attention. The Sunday brought some unexpected news: Victor Truscott had died suddenly of a heart attack. Webb felt a passing sadness, though no great surprise. It was obvious on his last visit that the old man had lost his will to live. Webb's sympathy was more with the unapproachable daughter. She would be very much alone.

Dr Stapleton phoned the next day. 'Thought you'd like to know I've done an autopsy on Truscott. No question that it was natural causes—a massive coronary. However, there's one point of interest. On a routine examination of the gastric contents we came across some undigested tablets. Since he was supposedly on no medication at the time of death, we investigated further and found a fairly high blood level of barbiturate. Not toxic, mind you, well within the therapeutic range, but a bit of a puzzle nonetheless. According to the local GP, Miss Truscott had a regular prescription for night sedation, so most probably the old boy suffered from insomnia and she gave him some of hers. It happens all the time, but I thought it worth mentioning.'

Webb was thoughtful as he replaced the receiver. He was remembering the self-reproach in the old man's voice as he admitted spending most of his time asleep. Perhaps even such a devoted daughter as Lana took liberties to gain some extra free-dom.

It wasn't till Wednesday evening that Webb's desk was clear enough to be left for a day with an easy conscience.

'Right, Ken,' he said wearily, rubbing his eyes with the heel of his palm, 'that's it. Tomorrow I'm incommunicado except in emergency. What have you got laid on?'

'I'm going back to Larksworth with Standing to check on a few loose ends.'

'Fine. I'll be in touch if I need you.'

His flat had the neglected look of somewhere that hadn't been lived in for a while. On the draining board stood an array of plates and glasses which, before falling into bed each night, he'd rinsed through. Now he stacked them together and put them away. He had just poured a neat whisky when the phone went. God, what now?

But it was Hannah's voice that reached him. 'I saw you garaging the car and thought you might welcome a hot meal. How does chilli sound?'

'Hot, certainly! Bless you, Hannah, that would be perfect. Give me half an hour. I need a soak to get rid of the aches.'

'Ready when you are, Guy!'

He nearly fell asleep in the bath, lying back while the hot water reddened his skin and lapped over his body in small, gentle caresses. His mind still circled round the murders, but it was an unprofitable circle, a cat chasing its own tail. Cat? His eyes flickered as he struggled after a thread of association which eluded him. Let it go. He was opting out tonight. Tomorrow, he told himself ironically, all would be revealed. God willing.

Hannah opened the door and he stood there simply holding her, his face in her hair, letting the calm of her soak into his mind. He knew that he owed her more than he was prepared to give, in consideration, in commitment. It was his good fortune that she dismissed the debt. She was content to accept him on his own terms and he acknowledged that he was luckier than he'd any right to be.

'You're exhausted, aren't you?' she said softly. 'Let's eat on trays by the fire.'

The chilli scorched his tongue, the accompanying lager cooled it. The warmth of the fire stole over him, the television made no demands. He was aware of Hannah gently removing his tray, and knew no more till he realized she was standing in front of him.

'Chief Inspector, sir, are you fit to return home or will you doss down here?'

'I doubt if I'd make the stairs,' he confessed shamefacedly.

He was soundly asleep when she came to bed. Later, in the night, he reached for her and, waking, she moved without question into his arms. Their brief, frenzied coming together was part of the restorative, and almost at once he slept again.

He woke finally to sunlight flooding in and the smell of frying bacon. Catching up his clothes, he padded naked to the bathroom. His mind was alive again, probing, sifting, already at work on the final deductions. For preference he'd have set out at once, without the distractions of social discourse, but he owed it to Hannah to eat the breakfast she'd prepared.

When he reached the kitchen she was crisping the frill round the fried eggs. 'Lucky I haven't a class till ten,' she remarked as he lifted her heavy hair and kissed the back of her neck.

'I'm almost there, Hannah. It's about to fall into shape.'

'Glad to hear it. They've been particularly nasty, these murders, like lightning out of a clear sky. No warning, no escape.'

It was a clear sky today, but condensation coated the window and, moving forward, Webb could see rime on the grass, the trees encrusted in frosting.

'I've filled a Thermos of soup for you,' Hannah told him, putting his plate on the table. 'And there's a couple of home-made rolls. Don't forget the inner man while you're cogitating, certainly when it's as cold as this.' She bent to kiss his cheek. 'I must go, love. Don't bother clearing away, I can see you're raring to be off. Happy hunting!'

The door of the flat closed behind her. For a few minutes longer Webb sat there, finishing his toast and draining the coffeepot. Then, taking her at her word, he rose from the table, leaving the empty dishes as they were, and let himself out of the flat.

The sun was strengthening as he drove down into Shillingham, and the rooftops glistened. The cold weather didn't bother him. He was warmly dressed and he welcomed its icy clarity. The whole white and blue day stretched ahead of him, his to do with as he willed. It didn't matter which direction he took. Shillingham's suburbs did not stretch far and it was surrounded by hills and woods where, without fear of disturbance, he could set up his easel and work out his puzzle. All the facts were there. He had only to juggle them into the right pattern.

Half an hour later he'd left the car and was starting out across the fields. He had trimmed his needs on these occasions to the

223

bare essentials—a folding stool, collapsible easel, the minimum of equipment. He walked for some time, falling naturally into a steady stride, feeling the strengthening sun on his head, the crunch of the grass under his feet. Though his ears were stinging with the cold, he scarcely noticed it.

Eventually he stopped and looked back. The field he had come up dropped away behind him, bordered by its spiky hedges and the gate through which he had come. A small outcrop of rock above him provided a windbreak. This would do admirably. He set up chair and easel, pinned on the paper, selected his charcoal, knowing from experience it was no use starting cold on his denouement. He'd begin by sketching the scene before him, letting his mind roam free till he was ready to commit it to paper. The time this preparation took varied from case to case. Sometimes he sketched for hours before facts and figures fell into place. Sometimes he'd barely started the first out-lines before he had to whip off the paper and start on a fresh sheet.

The facts, then, he thought, shading in the sweep of grass ahead of him. Five victims, all female, all taken unawares. Four divorcees, one unfaithful wife. No fingerprints. Only clue the pine needles and the minute pinpricks of blood. Jackson had checked the groups of everyone connected with the case. They were roughly one-third Group A, like Sylvia Dane, and two thirds 0, like her killer. And for those few enigmatic drops they were indebted to the small, terrified cat which had seen its mistress die. The cat.

Almost unconsciously, Webb stripped away the paper and fitted a new one, excitement building inside him. As was his custom, he first set the scene, drawing in everything connected in his mind with the various crimes. He'd been amused to read recently of a system known as 'Mind Maps' which was taught to businessmen. Basically, it was what he'd done for years, using a visual layout to coagulate his ideas.

He began with Linda Meadowes. The first appearance of the word Delilah and the discarded tube of lipstick. Alongside it he drew a moped and a pine tree, source of the few dried needles which had been trodden into the carpet. And the murder weapon, so far undiscovered; a rigid, short-bladed knife, designed to kill.

The first Broadminster death, that of Mrs Burke, he symbolized with a suitcase for the ill-fated holiday. There was a wood at the end of her road, but it was larches, not pines.

Now Jane Forbes: a loaf of bread and some teacups. Webb pictured the assailant at the table, watching as she filled the kettle, took the cups from the dresser; perhaps secretly fingering the blade of his weapon. Sick, evil. Yet he hadn't raped her. Why? Did he feel that would compound her infidelity, break faith with the wronged husband he avenged? Or was there another reason Webb had overlooked? Jackson had drawn a blank on homosexuals.

For a few minutes Webb let his mind circle the possibilities. Then, temporarily abandoning them, he progressed to Rose Percival in Otterford. For her he drew the candlestick that Bailey went to value. He *could* have returned on the Thursday, despite what he'd said. And he had the right blood group. As, Webb conceded, had two thirds of the population of Broadshire. More pine needles, and this time he could fit a rider to the moped, narrow-shouldered as Mrs Parker described.

So to Sylvia Dane. Webb sketched a rectangle for the painting commissioned by Paul Netherby. Then the cat, with arched back and glaring eyes. There was something about the cat, something he was overlooking. Frowningly he devoted some minutes to it, elaborating its outline with claws and whiskers. But without enlightenment. No pine needles here, and no moped. It seemed they went together.

Minutes ticked into hours as Webb doodled, mentally and physically. The paper was filling up. There were two market stalls for Otterford and Larksworth, three mopeds, only one of which had a rider, and no less than five daggers. Would they ever find that weapon? They couldn't search every house in the county.

Mowbray's sitting room came to mind, the portrait on the wall, the daggers by the fire. Any one of them would have fitted the bill. Left-handed, Mowbray said they were—a gratuitous piece of information. Or was it to throw them off the scent, since he himself was right-handed? For if Mowbray *were* the killer, what was to prevent his selecting a weapon from his own wall, using it to his purpose, and then replacing it? Webb remembered the tenseness, the silent challenge in the man when he showed an interest in the collection.

Experimentally he cast Mowbray as murderer and surveyed the possibilities. Like Bailey, he had the right blood group— and there were plenty of pine trees up the lane to his house! Momentarily Webb's grip tightened on the charcoal, then relaxed. Even if they found a moped on his premises, he could never be described as narrow-shouldered. Or were they placing too much importance on Mrs Parker's memory?

Motive? Well, his wife had left him. He could have been brooding for years, building up a paranoid hatred of faithless wives. Webb felt certain the victims were chosen as representatives of their kind, not from personal animosity. Their deaths were executions rather than crimes of passion. Mowbray was capable of that detached callousness, and he'd been in the area when Mrs Dane died. In that instance, at least, he'd had motive, means, and opportunity.

Almost with reluctance, Webb sketched in the items sent to Kate Romilly. Yet if he dismissed her skinhead theory—and to them, one frightened woman would be of only passing interest—the most likely sender was the murderer. But why the change of operation? Up to now, he had struck without warning.

Thoughtfully he retraced the latest outlines, embroidering the moth's thorax with its sinister and disregarded skull. What was the motive behind it? Escalating terror, ending in death, or an escape clause? Suppose the killer knew Kate, was reluctant to carry out what he felt to be his duty. Might he not try by this harassment to frighten her back to her husband and consequent safety?

Webb reached for Hannah's basket. The soup sent warmth coursing through him, though he'd been unaware of cold, and the rolls satisfied a hunger he hadn't recognized. He ate quickly, his eyes moving over the drawings, and, brushing the crumbs from his trousers, returned to work. The background was as complete as he could make it. Now the actors must be brought on stage.

A few deft strokes caught the traits which identified each figure. Mowbray, exaggeratedly squat, with thick hair and vacant eyes; Kate's dark, frightened gaze and Bailey's unconvincing charm. Then Lana Truscott's gaunt face and home-knitted sweater, and Henry Dane, peering through spectacles at his changed world. The figures multiplied: Netherby, Mrs Parker, the pathologist—all who, suspects or not, had walked briefly onto the murder stage must take their places in the finale.

The canvas was complete, and hidden in it, he knew, lay the solution to the case. Somehow, by a narrowing of concentration on each symbol in turn, he must hope for a slight shift in focus which would give a new slant. And already something was stirring. That Sunday he'd spent with Fleming: he'd felt at the time he'd missed something.

His eyes moved systematically across the sheet as his mind reached backwards, both locking at the same instant on the drawing of a pine tree. Where had he recently looked out of a window and—?

He straightened, excitement pricking his scalp. He'd gazed down a length of garden to a gate opening on pinewoods. From Victor Truscott's bedroom. Suppose there'd been a more sinister reason for his daughter's doctoring him with pills? Webb had accepted they'd extend her freedom, but to do what?

All but one murder was committed in the afternoon. Lana Truscott worked at the shop mornings only. And the old man had said something he hadn't latched on to at the time: 'Lana's allergic to cats.'

To cats! Lana, sneezing and red-eyed, rubbing her arm as though the coarse wool irritated her skin. Or was the irritation not from the wool but in the skin itself, a rash which, taken with her sneezing, pointed to allergy rather than the cold she'd mentioned? And only three days earlier, the Danes' cat had clawed a killer.

Webb reined in his racing thoughts. They'd need more proof than that. The pine needles and the cat slotted into place. What of the moped? Hadn't—his mouth was dry—hadn't Ralph Truscott driven one to his death in the river? Suppose it hadn't been sold but kept in that shed he'd noticed in the back garden?

If, to avoid notice, it were wheeled through the back gate into the wood and across the fields, the rider's shoes would collect some needles. Mrs Parker assumed the rider was a youth: because, small and slight, the figure was in fact more like a woman?

So Lana Truscott, like Mowbray, had the opportunity— long, lonely afternoons while her invalid father slept. What of motive and means? Webb cast his mind back, remembering that when Ralph Truscott died, his sister's grief had outweighed his estranged wife's. And the broken marriage, following on illness and redundancy, had been the catalyst that led to suicide. Did she, in a crazed, one-woman campaign, feel she was avenging him, even—my God!—Richard Mowbray, to whom she seemed devoted and whose wife had also left him?

Baffled, Webb shook his head. He'd never understand the tortuous twistings of the human psyche. Still, he'd established motive and opportunity. What of the weapon? Mowbray was unlikely to loan her his.

Then he drew in his breath. He'd facetiously imagined Mowbray using and replacing his own weapons, but there were also daggers at Pennyfarthings! Suppose Lana Truscott had done precisely that, and the murder weapon had literally been in front of their noses all the time?

Though not quite all the time. And during its absence, wouldn't Kate or the partners have missed it? It seemed an unacceptable risk to take. Momentarily shelving that question, Webb returned to the motive. Lana would know Mrs Dane's reputation, and consider it as guilty as desertion. And she'd been babysitting for Kate Romilly on the night of her murder, a mere hundred yards from the Danes' house! No wonder the moped and pine needles weren't in evidence. If he was right, the murderer came in by bus—and was considerately driven home in a police car!

There was still the question of why the victims admitted Lana. Possibly she'd posed as a market researcher. But once having let her in, they wouldn't expect attack from another woman.

And the packages. His second alternative seemed correct. Lana liked Kate, didn't want to harm her. Yet she had left her husband, a 'crime' that couldn't be ignored. If she could be frightened back to him, she would also be removed from Mowbray's orbit. For should Kate, having left Michael, become involved with Richard, she'd be twice damned and nothing could save her.

And she was still in danger, danger which, like the five women before her, she had no means of recognizing.

Webb reached for his radio, calling the control room to instruct all units to be on the lookout for Lana Truscott. 'Please God she's safely at home,' he finished briskly. 'I'm on my way to Littlemarsh now. Send a backup, will you, to wait out of sight till I get there. Oh, and if you can catch Romilly at the *News*, tell him to go to his wife. She might need his support.'

He bundled his belongings together and started back to the car at a run.

CHAPTER 22

'But I'm glad you called, Lana,' Kate said warmly. 'It must be very lonely at home.'

Lana was standing in the middle of the room, gauche, out of place, her face white above the dark navy of her coat.

'Give me your coat and sit down,' Kate prompted. The woman lowered herself into a chair but made no attempt to remove the garment. Her eyes as she looked up at Kate were unfocused, as though, Kate thought uncomfortably, she was looking at something else. But she'd been devoted to her father; no wonder she was in a state of shock.

Briefly Kate thought of Mary Lucas upstairs. Lana's ring at the door had coincided with a radio signal from outside telling them who the caller was. In keeping with instructions, Mary had left Kate to greet her visitor alone.

'They cut him up,' Lana was saying jerkily. 'Just because he hadn't seen the doctor.' She shuddered, her whole body racked with the spasm.

'It's for the death certificate. They can't issue one if—'

'They did the same to Ralph. The one who should have

been cut up was Sandra. She killed them both.'

'Try not to think that, Lana. I know it must seem that way, but—'

'When Ralph died, Father—' She broke off, staring down at her twisting hands. 'Father said, "If Sandra walked in now, I'd strangle her with my bare hands."'

'But he didn't mean it. It's the kind of thing people do say in moments of stress.'

'He meant it,' Lana said simply.

Kate's eyes fell from the mindless gaze and she tried to change the subject. 'Did you find your cheque-book?'

Lana looked at her blankly.

'When you went down to look. Was it in your desk?'

'Oh, yes. Yes.'

It was going to be a difficult afternoon. A full hour yet before Josh would be home. Had she locked the front door when Lana arrived? Almost certainly not. Her face through the glass had put it out of her mind. Still, the police guard was across the road.

'I'll make a cup of tea,' she said brightly.

'No. There isn't time.'

Kate, about to rise, hesitated in surprise. 'You're leaving already?'

Lana didn't seem to have heard her. She said harshly, 'Don't worry about Josh. I'll look after him.'

Kate stared at her, the pinprick of unease deepening.

'I love Josh, Kate. You know that. He wasn't meant to find the mouse. I'd have given anything, to spare him that.'

'But it wasn't your—' Kate broke off, coldness spreading inside her.

'I saved the pigeon till I knew he was in bed.'

'Lana, you're surely not saying—?'

'And I labelled it, so you wouldn't think it was from those boys.' Her mouth twisted in the parody of a smile. 'You're not easy to frighten, Kate. I tried so hard to send you back to your husband. So hard.'

Kate said very carefully. 'What else did you do?'

Lana moved her hands an inch or so. 'The phone calls, the man on the bench. There wasn't really anyone.'

'But I saw him,' Kate insisted through dry lips.

'He happened to be there when I arrived for work. I'd never seen him before.' She met Kate's bewildered eyes and added plaintively, 'Why do you make me do this? You're my friend, but you're harming Josh and I can't let you. We must stamp out permissiveness, or one day he'll be hurt as badly as Ralph, and—and Richard.' Her face glowed briefly as she spoke his name, the first time Kate had heard her use it.

Kate said with an effort. 'You're confused, Lana. It's not surprising, all the murders and then your father's death. But try not to worry. The police are after a man with red hair, and when they find him it will all be over.'

'There isn't any man.' Lana fumbled in her handbag and drew out a dagger. Kate recognized it. It was the smaller of the Indian kards. 'This is what I went down for. Neat, isn't it? It fits into the hilt of the large one, so it's never missed.'

Afterwards, Kate couldn't explain why she hadn't called Mary. True, a scream might have provoked attack, but it never even occurred to her. Quite simply, she couldn't accept that Lana would hurt her. All the same, she needed humouring.

'You're right, Lana.' She strove to keep her voice level. 'I shouldn't have left Michael. I'll go back to him, I promise.'

Lana looked confused. 'But it's too late.'

Wilfully, Kate misunderstood. 'It's never too late. Think how happy Josh will be!'

Lana made a low sound in her throat, half pain, half anger. 'If you'd said that last week—yesterday—' She rose clumsily to her feet, her handbag sliding unnoticed to the floor. Kate rose with her, eyes on the gleaming blade.

Lana said shakily, 'It won't hurt. You won't feel—'

Everything happened at once. There was a cry and the sound of feet overhead, a crash downstairs as the front door rocked open. The two women stood frozen as footsteps came running down one flight of stairs, up the other. From behind her, Kate heard Michael's voice: 'Kate! Oh my God!' and superimposed on it, another: 'All right, Miss Truscott, you can drop that now.'

The silence stretched like elastic, snapped as Mary Lucas said, 'Cover me, Jack. I'll try—'

Lana moved suddenly, arm upraised. Michael yelled, '*Down, Kate!*' and she flung herself sideways to the floor. But the dagger was not after all intended for her. With a choked cry Lana drove it into her breast and fell forward as the detective ran to catch her.

Kate lay where she had fallen till Michael pulled her to her feet.

'You're all right? She didn't touch you?'

Kate's eyes were drawn in glazed fascination to the figure on the floor. Mary Lucas, feeling swiftly for a pulse, looked up at her colleague and shook her head.

'Should we try resuscitation?'

'No point, Jack. She knew where to aim—she's had plenty of practice.' Mary straightened, turned to Kate. 'Thank God you're OK. The message only just came through. I've never moved so fast in my life!'

Kate moistened her lips. 'Is Lana dead?'

'Yes. Best thing, really.' Mary stooped and closed the staring eyes.

Kate said on a rising note, 'Oh God!' The shaking had started, rattling her teeth. In the distance she could hear police sirens, growing louder.

Mary said gently, 'It's over, Kate. Would you like me to take you upstairs?'

'Don't bother.' Michael's arm tightened round Kate's shoulder. 'She's coming home with me. Aren't you, Kate?'

She turned her head, meeting the anxious question in his eyes. 'Yes,' she confirmed. 'I'm going home.'

After all, she had promised Lana.

Milton Keynes UK
Ingram Content Group UK Ltd.
UKHW040629301023
431584UK00004B/172